Mac scowled at

The thought of leaving the hospital without seeing for himself that A.J. was okay was unsettling. And disturbing.

Unease slid through him. He'd kept the same vigil for other colleagues. He'd consumed countless cups of undrinkable hospital coffee, paced waiting rooms more times than he'd liked.

But he'd never felt the terror he'd experienced when he saw A.J. lying on the pavement. And never before had he volunteered to ride in the ambulance with an injured colleague.

It was the situation, he told himself. It was because the perp was Doak Talbott and he wanted the man so badly.

He leaned against the wall and stared at the doors to the E.R. He had to stay. It was his duty.

Dear Reader,

Trust is the essence of any relationship, whether it is between friends, lovers or spouses. In order to give freely of yourself, you must be able to trust that your partner will never betray you, never judge you, never abandon you.

But what if you have something in your past that you've hidden from the world, something that is the very antithesis of what your loved one stands for? How do you gather your courage to tell him the truth about yourself? How do you stand in front of him, fully exposed, waiting for his reaction?

And what about the person on the receiving end of those revelations? How would he feel, knowing that his partner withheld parts of herself, afraid he wouldn't be able to deal with them? How do you rebuild trust once it is shattered?

With their pasts and their baggage, A. J. Ferguson and Mac McDougal should never have fallen in love. But sometimes the heart doesn't pay attention to the mind. Sometimes the heart knows exactly what it wants, in spite of the obstacles. And sometimes, if you listen to your heart, you find the person who is the missing piece of the puzzle, the person who makes you whole.

I love the characters in all the books I've written. But once in a great while, as I sit in front of my computer, magic happens. The characters I'm writing about leap off the screen and sit next to me. They become so real, so much a part of my life, that they walk beside me as I go through my day and whisper to me at night while I dream. A.J. and Mac are two of the magic people. I hope you enjoy reading their story as much as I enjoyed writing it.

I love to hear from my readers. You can contact me at mwatson1004@hotmail.com or visit my Web site at www.margaretwatson.com.

Margaret Watson

IN HER DEFENSE
Margaret Watson

HARLEQUIN®

TORONTO • NEW YORK • LONDON
AMSTERDAM • PARIS • SYDNEY • HAMBURG
STOCKHOLM • ATHENS • TOKYO • MILAN • MADRID
PRAGUE • WARSAW • BUDAPEST • AUCKLAND

ISBN 0-373-71288-X

IN HER DEFENSE

Copyright © 2005 by Margaret Watson.

This edition published by arrangement with Harlequin Books S.A.

® and TM are trademarks of the publisher. Trademarks indicated with
® are registered in the United States Patent and Trademark Office, the
Canadian Trade Marks Office and in other countries.

www.eHarlequin.com

Printed in U.S.A.

Books by Margaret Watson

HARLEQUIN SUPERROMANCE
1205–TWO ON THE RUN
1258–HOMETOWN GIRL

For Lindsay Longford and Julie Wachowski,
my fabulous, insightful and wise story conferencing buddies.
Thanks for all the gentle nudges in the right direction.

And thanks to Joan Andresen
for sharing her martial arts expertise.

CHAPTER ONE

"DAMN IT, FERGUSON, I don't have time for this!"

A. J. Ferguson watched Pierce McDougal storm into her office, stopping in front of her desk. His blue eyes flashed with anger and his body language screamed furious cop.

"You're the victim's advocate for the Riverton Police Department," he said. "You're supposed to be helping the victims of crimes deal with the system. You're not supposed to be helping them *avoid* the system! I need to talk to Mindy Talbott. Right now."

A.J. sat up straight in her chair and narrowed her eyes at him. "That's too bad, Detective McDougal. Mindy already told you she doesn't know where her husband went. I will not take you to see her right now. She doesn't need to be bullied."

"I am not going to bully her." McDougal spoke slowly, his voice rising with each word. "I am trying to protect her. Is that such a difficult concept for you to grasp?"

"You won't be protecting her if you go to the safe house and confront her. Mindy needs peace and quiet."

McDougal loomed over her. His broad shoulders blocked out the overhead fluorescent light, and his dark shadow covered her desk. But he said nothing more.

Two could play this game of intimidation. A.J. stood. At almost six feet, she could look most of the police officers in the department in the eye.

McDougal straightened without dropping his gaze. He was a full head taller.

A.J. leaned toward McDougal until her face was inches away from his. "You don't scare me, Detective. And you're not going to frighten Mindy. She's had enough of that from her husband."

"For God's sake, Ferguson." He stepped away from her desk and ran his hand through his hair. The dark waves stood at attention. "I'm trying to help her. She's not going to be safe until we put Doak Talbott behind bars. And we can't do that unless she tells us where he is."

"You asked her last night."

"Last night she'd been beaten and she'd watched her son get slapped around. I'm hoping she'll have some ideas today."

"I don't think she knows, Mac."

"And even if she did, she wouldn't testify against him anyway."

A.J. didn't answer. He was right. Mindy wouldn't press charges against her husband, no matter how badly he beat her. She was too afraid of what would happen when he got out of jail.

And he *would* get out of jail. Men like Doak Talbott didn't languish in jail. Their smooth-talking attorneys in designer suits made sure of that. The familiar anger burned her chest, hardening her resolve. She *would* keep Mindy and her son, Jamie, safe.

"Where's the kid?" McDougal asked, his voice weary.

"With DCFS. They took him to a foster home until Mindy's sister can get here."

The detective closed his eyes, and A.J. saw him reaching for his composure. When he opened them again, the anger had leached away.

"We're not on opposite sides here, Ferguson. We want the same thing—that scumbag Talbott locked up. If I promise to be a good boy, will you let me talk to Mindy?"

He flashed a strained version of his famous smile at her, and her stomach fluttered. The dimple in his right cheek deepened and he leaned closer again. "I know how to play nice. Women like me, Ferguson."

That was the understatement of the century, if even a fraction of the rumors she'd heard were true. Struggling with her own composure, she said, "I'll ask her if she's willing to talk to you. That's my best offer."

"Be sure and tell her what a kind, considerate, soft-spoken guy I am."

She snorted. "Even I don't have the nerve to tell a lie that big, McDougal."

His smile faded. "I don't care what you tell her. I want Talbott, and she's the only lead I have."

"I'll talk to her."

"Right now."

"When I get a chance," she retorted. "She's not the only victim who needs my help."

"What else have you got? No, wait, I remember. You have to give support and counseling to that moron who went into the Indian Park neighborhood to buy crack and got knocked around and robbed at gunpoint."

A.J. flushed. "Just because he showed a lack of good judgment doesn't mean he deserved to be attacked. At least he's trying to straighten himself out. He made an appointment with me and I'm not going to cancel it. He's on his way here right now."

"You're going to put Doak Talbott on the back burner while you counsel some idiot addict?" His voice filled with incredulity.

"I'm Riverton's only victim's advocate, Detective." Her voice dripped ice. "I don't pick and choose which victims are worthy of my help. My office door is open to anyone who needs me."

"That's your problem, Ferguson. You bleeding hearts are all the same. You open a vein for any schmuck who walks in the door, and the blood loss has affected your brain. You need to get your priorities straight."

The cowering child she'd been flashed in her memory. "My priorities are just fine, thank you very much." She raised her eyebrows. It was time to go on the attack. "Is Mindy your only lead? You've been looking at Doak Talbott for a while, haven't you? For that waitress from the country club who disappeared? Surely a decorated detective like you would have developed other sources to question."

His face tightened and cold anger was in his eyes. "You know damn well that the country-club set takes care of their own. You think one of his friends is going to give him up?"

She looked away. He was right, and she knew it. Doak Talbott's friends would deny any knowledge of his whereabouts, even if Doak were standing right next to them.

"All right. I'll go see Mindy tonight," she said. "If she's willing to talk to you, we'll go to the shelter tomorrow. But I'm not going to press her."

"Fine. Get in touch with me as soon as she agrees to see me."

"Don't worry, McDougal. I know how to do my job. I suggest you go out and do yours. Figure out where Doak Talbott is."

"That's why I need to talk to your client, Ferguson. If you want him caught, you know where to find me."

The floor shook beneath her feet with the force of the slamming door.

"SOMEONE IS GOING TO WRING Ferguson's neck one of these days," McDougal snarled to his partner as he threw himself into his desk chair. "And right now, I'd have to call it justifiable homicide."

Jake Donovan looked over at him. "Another run-in with our victim's advocate?"

"That woman takes the meaning of stubborn to a whole new level."

"So which order of yours did she refuse to follow?"

Mac scowled at him and crossed his arms over his chest. "Very funny, Donovan. You're a real comedian."

"You could try making nice with A.J. She's a smart, savvy woman. No one in the department wants to nail the bad guys more than she does. Use some of that famous McDougal charm on her."

"That woman is un-charm-able."

Jake raised his eyebrows. "There's an actual living, breathing woman who can resist Mac McDougal? Did you flash that dimple at her? Or flutter your baby blues in her direction?"

"Knock it off, Donovan. You might have time for chitchat, but I've got scumbags to catch."

He reached for the pile of file folders on his desk and began flipping through one randomly. Ferguson's refusal to let him talk to Mindy Talbott really pissed him off. Doak Talbott was at the top of Mac's list right now. He wanted to toss the rich SOB into a cell and slam the door himself. Not only had Talbott beaten his wife and kid, but he was the prime suspect in the disappearance of Helena Tripp, a young waitress who'd gone missing from the country club ten days ago. But being questioned by the cops didn't rattle him. Why should it? The wealthy real-estate developer had always used his money and his influence to shield himself from accountability.

"He laughed at us," Mac said in a low voice, staring at the file in front of him but seeing Doak Talbott's sneering face. "The last time we went to his house, the bastard laughed at us."

"We'll find him." Jake eased his chair back. "We've got flags on all his accounts and we've already sent out descriptions of his car. He won't get far."

"You know how it works, Jake." Mac stared at his partner, fury raging through him. "He'll get another car. He'll have accounts we don't even know about. He'll have friends who will help him, no questions asked. We're spinning our wheels."

"The man's not a rocket scientist, Mac." Jake's voice was mild. "He's just a rich guy with resources. We have resources, too."

"Guys like Talbott always slither out of charges against them. You know it as well as I do. They're made of Teflon. Nothing sticks to them."

"Is this pity party almost over? Because it's bringing a little tear to my eye, and I don't want to embarrass myself in front of the rest of the guys."

"Up yours, Donovan." Mac spoke without heat. He glanced at the door to A.J.'s office and let his anger dissipate. "Ferguson brings out the worst in me."

"You're just touchy because she won't melt into a puddle at your feet."

"Ferguson doesn't melt," Mac said. "She stares at you as if you're a bug on a dissection tray. And she's looking forward to sticking in the pins."

"Do I detect a hint of sour grapes here? Is it possible you've tried to work your wiles on the lovely A. J. Ferguson and been shut down?"

"With a body like that, who wouldn't be tempted?" Mac said. Not to mention her generous mouth and dark, seductive eyes. "But I've learned at least a couple of things in my thirty-three years. And one of them is 'don't mess with women you work with.'"

"You're a wise man, son. Nothing will bring you trouble faster." Jake glanced at the clock. "Weren't you heading over to the country club?"

"Tomorrow. I'm going to catch them at lunch."

"You need some help?"

"Nah. They're not going to give anything away. But I have to try."

"I guess they're not susceptible to your charm, either."

"Go to hell, Donovan," he said, but he grinned as he got to his feet. "Better me than you. They don't need your ugly puss scaring away the members."

A.J. RUBBED HER FOREHEAD as the door closed behind the client who'd kept her from talking to Mindy Talbott.

As much as she hated to admit it, McDougal was right.
The client was an idiot. He'd driven his expensive car
into the worst neighborhood in Riverton, then flashed
a wad of cash while he bought his drugs. No wonder
he'd ended up on the business end of a gun.

But he'd chosen to come talk to her. The man realized he had a problem, and she respected him for that.

She'd referred him to a substance-abuse rehabilita-
tion program, as well as a private therapist. After scribbling a note to herself to call her colleague and fill her
in, she pushed away from her desk and reached for her
handbag. It was after five, but she had to visit Mindy
Talbott. She'd promised McDougal she'd talk to the
woman.

And she always kept her promises.

Heat shimmered off the asphalt as she drove through
downtown. The small boutiques and funky shops that
catered to the college students gave way to a residen-
tial neighborhood, and the tree-lined streets shaded her
car, protecting it from the glare of the sun. The air
smelled fresher in this part of town, cleaner, as if the
residents had erected a barrier against the run-down
apartments and shabby houses only a few blocks away.

Neat middle-class homes lined the streets, all of
them well tended and cared for. The safe house was a
few blocks over, tucked into the middle of a block and
looking exactly like all the other homes.

A stoplight brought her to a halt, and as she waited

for the light to change, awareness prickled at the back of her neck. Someone was watching her.

A.J. glanced in the rearview mirror. The vehicle behind her was a minivan, and as A.J. watched, the young woman driving the van whipped her head around. Her body language said she wasn't happy with the passengers.

In the lane next to the van, a teenager bobbed his head and danced his shoulders, moving to the beat of music.

Neither of them so much as glanced at her.

When the light changed, she shot into the intersection and turned the corner. Three cars followed her. She didn't recognize any of them.

By the time she'd taken several more corners, only one of the cars was left behind her. It was a battered, mud-colored sedan. The antenna bent outward at a ninety-degree angle and the front bumper was attached with duct tape. She kept her eye on it, not relaxing until she turned another corner and the car continued down the street. She drove around the block a couple of times, but there was no sign of the car.

She was just jumpy from her run-in with McDougal, she told herself. She prided herself on her ability to take control of any situation, but she never quite managed to control Mac.

Mac McDougal was testosterone on the hoof, a walking advertisement for cool sheets and hot sex. No wonder most women drooled when he walked by. Thank goodness she was immune to his charm.

By the time she'd parked and walked to the safe house, her heart rate was back to normal. She rang the bell and waited while the video camera above the door recorded her face and relayed it to a monitor inside the house.

Finally the door opened and a woman with faded blond hair and gentle eyes gave her a tired smile. "Hi, A.J. What's up?"

"Hello, Jenny. I need to talk to Mindy Talbott."

The woman glanced up the stairs. "She hasn't come out of her room all day. Do you want me to get her?"

"No, I'll go up. We'll have more privacy in her room."

"Go ahead. She's in room three."

"Thanks."

The floors at Harbor House were scuffed and the walls held the handprints of too many children. Jenny tried to make the shelter cheerful, with bright pictures on the walls and vases of flowers in every room, but A.J. shivered as the front door closed behind her.

Misery clung to the walls of the house, and the air was permeated with the smells of disinfectant and despair. A.J. battled her urge to escape the pain as she headed up the stairs.

Children's voices floated up to her from the family room in the back of the house. They almost brought an air of normality to the atmosphere.

Almost.

No wonder Mindy didn't want to come downstairs. The children would be a painful reminder of her own son, taken away from her and now in foster care.

She knocked softly, not wanting to startle Mindy. There was absolute silence on the other side of the door. Finally, when she knocked again, a small voice said, "Who is it?"

"It's A. J. Ferguson, Mrs. Talbott. The victim's advocate from the police station. We met last night."

The silence stretched too long before Mindy said, "What do you want?"

"I need to talk to you. Do you want to talk in your room or come downstairs?"

After a long pause, the door opened. Mindy Talbott's blond hair was tangled around her face and flattened on one side, as if she hadn't bothered to comb it after she got up. The left side of her face was swollen and mottled with bruises, and the white of her eye was shockingly red with blood. A line of stitches stretched from her lip to her chin.

Shame, fear and grief filled the woman's eyes.

"Is it Jamie?" she whispered. "Is he all right?"

"Jamie's fine," A.J. answered, making a mental note to check on the boy. "Your sister is on her way here to take care of him."

A.J. waited by the door as Mindy stared at her. One of the children on the first floor shouted up the stairs, and she shrunk into herself.

"Is it all right if I come in?" A.J. asked quietly.

Mindy nodded her head and moved away. A.J. slipped inside and closed the door behind her, muffling the noise from below.

"What do you want?" Mindy asked.

"Why don't you sit down?" A.J. answered. She waited until the woman lowered herself carefully into the easy chair, then perched on the bed.

"How are you feeling?"

Mindy stared at her, a spark of hostility in her eyes. "I feel like I'm in prison. Like I'm being punished."

Thank God Mindy could at least feel angry. "Harbor House is a safe place to be," A.J. answered. "Doak can't hurt you here. He doesn't even know where you are."

"You took my baby away."

"We had to," A.J. said gently. "Doak had been abusing Jamie. And…"

"And I let him. That's what they told me last night." Mindy's forehead wrinkled as she stared at A.J. "But what could I do? Doak is stronger than I am. I couldn't stop him."

Hot anger rose like lava inside A.J., overwhelming, consuming anger. Excuses. They all made excuses. She wanted to scream at Mindy that mothers were supposed to protect their children. Even if the abusers turned on them.

Instead she gripped her hands together in her lap so

hard that her fingernails cut into her palms. She couldn't judge the woman in front of her. She knew the psychology of domestic abuse, knew how it destroyed the soul and crushed the spirit. She knew only too well what Mindy faced. Struggling to keep her voice calm, she said, "The police want to come and talk to you about Doak. Would that be all right?"

The woman's spark of anger disappeared, replaced by deep fear. "No," she whispered. "I can't. He told me he would kill me if I ever went to the police. I believe him. He'll kill both me and Jamie."

"We'll protect you, Mindy. We won't let him hurt you. But we need to find him. And we need your help to do it."

"Who would I have to talk to?"

A.J. drew an unsteady breath at this first sign of surrender and forced herself to go slowly. "One of the detectives who came to your house last night. Detectives McDougal and Donovan."

"The tall one?"

"That's McDougal." No matter what their circumstances, women remembered Mac.

Mindy twisted her hands in her lap, pleating the material of her slacks between shaking fingers. "Are you sure Doak doesn't know where I am?"

"Positive," she answered. "The location of this house is a well-kept secret. There's no way he could find out."

"Doak has ways of finding out anything he wants to find out."

"Not this."

A.J. held Mindy's gaze until the woman looked away. "All right. I'll talk to that detective."

"I'll bring him by tomorrow. Is that all right?" A.J. was careful to give Mindy a choice. Victims of domestic abuse often had no choices in their lives.

"I suppose."

"Is there anything I can do for you?"

"Give Jamie back to me."

"I can't do that right now. Soon, I hope." After Mindy had taken a parenting class and entered therapy. And Doak Talbott was no longer a danger to either of them.

"Then there's nothing you can do for me."

A.J. stood up and moved to the chair, crouching in front of the woman. "I gave you my card with my phone numbers. Do you still have it?"

Mindy nodded.

"Call me anytime, even if you just want to talk. All right?" She waited for Mindy to nod. "I'll see you tomorrow." A.J. glanced at her watch. "Jenny will be serving dinner in a few minutes. You must be hungry."

Mindy shook her head. "I don't want anything."

A.J. stood at the door, wishing she had a magic wand. She'd wave it over Mindy Talbott and make her whole again. She'd give her strength and self-esteem and a healed soul.

She closed the door behind her. There was no such thing as a magic wand.

She ought to know. She'd spent her childhood searching for one. And the only thing she'd found was pain, humiliation and guilt.

CHAPTER TWO

A BLAST OF HOT AIR greeted A.J. when she opened the door to her car. Shivering, she slid onto the seat, grateful for the warmth.

She was always cold when she left the shelter. The hopelessness of the residents burrowed into her bones, consuming all the heat inside her.

She wanted only to go home to her apartment, to fix dinner, have a glass of wine and unwind. But she had to go back to the office first. She'd forgotten a stack of case files she needed to work on tonight.

The trees dotting the parking lot outside the police station cast grotesque shadows onto the pavement. Dusk was creeping in, sharpening the air and bringing the welcome bite of a breeze off Lake Michigan.

She sighed as she got out of the car and hurried toward the lights of the building. Why hadn't she remembered to take the files when she'd left earlier?

She knew why. Mac McDougal. The man had rattled her, and she hated that she'd let him.

A.J. burst through the door, her long strides carrying her past the large room that held the detectives' desks. Normally an animated swirl of movement, ringing telephones and loud voices, tonight the bull pen was deserted except for Jake Donovan. He was hunched over his desk, telephone propped between shoulder and ear, scribbling on a pad of paper. He gave her a distracted wave as she hurried into her office. It took only a minute to scoop up the folders she'd left on her desk. Then, scanning her neat office, making sure everything was in its place, she stepped out and closed the door behind her.

"Hey there, A.J."

Jake dropped the receiver back in its cradle, looped his hands behind his head and gave her a lazy grin. Her mouth curved in an answering smile. She'd always liked McDougal's easygoing partner.

It had helped that he was one of the few men on the force who hadn't eyed her like a side of beef when she'd joined the department.

Neither had McDougal. But Jake didn't push her buttons. McDougal was a master at it.

"Hey yourself, Jake. What are you doing here so late?"

"Cleaning up after Mac. Trying to make him look good, as usual. I'm afraid it's a lost cause."

"Then don't stay too late. There'll be plenty of work left for you to do tomorrow."

Jake laughed and leaned forward in his chair. "Did you get a chance to talk to Mindy Talbott?"

"I just came from the shelter. I'll take McDougal there tomorrow."

"Good job, A.J. Another win for the good guys."

"Not yet, I'm afraid. Do you have any ideas where Doak is hiding?"

Jake's smile vanished. "Not a one. The dirt ball is gone. Nobody's heard from him."

"Maybe Mindy will have some ideas."

"You think so?"

No, she didn't. The woman was so traumatized she barely remembered her own name. "I hope so."

"Take it easy, A.J.," Jake called as she left.

"You, too, Jake," she answered over her shoulder.

The station door latched behind her with a solid click as she stepped into the cooling air of the evening. The shadows were longer now and the sky had darkened to royal blue. Tucking the folders under her arm, she headed toward her car in the deserted lot, fishing her keys out of her purse as she walked.

Without warning, an arm slipped around her neck and yanked her back into the hard wall of a male body.

Fear rolled in her stomach and bile rose in her throat. "No," she gasped, struggling to get the word past the cruel tightness crushing her throat. This would not happen to her. She would not allow it.

Folders scattered and her purse went flying as she struggled for leverage. But her moment of frozen panic had cost her. As she scrabbled to position herself to throw her attacker over her shoulder, his arm flexed cru-elly, and she was lifted off the ground. She kicked back, aiming for his knee, but he squeezed her neck harder.

"Bitch!" He growled into her ear, his breath hot on her neck. "You took them away from me." Something stabbed into her side, burning like a hot poker. "You stole them. You stinking bitch!"

"Wha-what are you talking about?" she managed to say, clawing at the arm around her neck. It was a steel band, unflinching and unmoving. Her vision began to gray.

"You know what I'm talking about." He pulled her toward the line of bushes around the building. "You sent the police to my house. My *house*. You got to that bitch Mindy and now you're going to pay."

"Doak?" she asked. Ice-cold terror mushroomed inside her. She clawed again at his arm as he dragged her, and she realized her key chain was still looped over her wrist.

She grabbed a key and stabbed it backward, aiming for his eyes. The sharp edge slid off the side of his face. Instead of disabling him, it made him howl with fury.

"I'm going to kill you, bitch!" he panted. His other hand shifted in front of her, holding something that glittered in the streetlight.

She struggled with her keys, searching for the re-mote opener. Finally she grasped it and managed to press every button.

The sound of a car horn ripped through the silence,

short blasts repeated over and over. Thank God for panic buttons.

"Give me that." He reached for the keys, but A.J. drew her arm back and threw them as far as she could. The alarm continued its relentless warning.

Talbott's arm tightened even more, cutting the trickle of air to almost nothing. A.J. kicked out again. She would not lose control.

Far away a car door slammed, and she felt Talbott's attention shift. "I'll be back, bitch. This isn't over. And next time I'll finish what we started."

Talbott pushed her from him, and A.J. staggered, falling onto the asphalt. Footsteps pounded on the pavement, coming closer. She rolled onto her stomach, gulping air. She tried to stand up, but her legs refused to hold her. The pavement was warm beneath her cheek and she pressed closer, trying to banish the cold that penetrated to her bones.

"Ferguson?" A voice spoke above her, and a hand touched her arm. She flinched away, fear rushing through her.

"It's okay, A.J. It's Mac." She felt him crouching next to her. "What the hell happened?"

Mac McDougal. She struggled to sit up, but he stopped her with a hand on her shoulder. He leaned closer and his scent swirled around her, a mix of soap, sweat and evening air. He skimmed a hand over her side, his fingers lingering for a long moment, and he said, "Lie still."

He ordered over his shoulder, "Call an ambulance."

"Already done," another voice, Jake's, answered.

"No ambulance," she whispered. "I'm okay."

"Shut up." Mac's shadow blocked out the light. "Just hold still."

"I'm okay," she insisted, struggling to roll over so she could get to her feet.

"No, you're not." A gentle hand brushed her hair away from her face. "But you're going to be fine."

Mac's eyes were calm and reassuring, and suddenly she wanted to reach out and grab hold of him. Her fingers brushed his arm, then quickly pulled back.

"D-did Talbott get away?" she asked, her teeth beginning to chatter with the cold.

"Doak Talbott did this?" Rage darkened the blue of Mac's eyes until they looked black.

"I—I think so. He s-said something about M-Mindy." Convulsive shivers wracked her body, and she couldn't stop the chattering.

"Get a blanket. Then call patrol," Mac ordered, and someone murmured into a radio. "Arrogant bastard. Attacking you here. We'll find him."

The wail of an ambulance siren grew steadily louder, and A.J. tried to sit up. She didn't want to go to the hospital.

"Don't move." Mac held her down. His hand was gentle but unyielding. "Every time you try to get up you bleed."

"I'm bleeding?" she asked. She touched her throat. It burned and throbbed, but she couldn't feel any blood.

"You've got a cut in your side. Did he have a knife?"

"He cut me?" she asked, feeling slow and stupid. Her brain wasn't working right.

Mac's face softened as he looked down at her. "Just lie still, A.J. The medics are almost here." He tucked something warm around her, something that smelled like Mac. A sweater.

"I don't need an ambulance." She tried to push the sweater away, but her hands wouldn't cooperate.

"Don't you ever give up? You're lying in a pool of blood and you're still giving orders." But his eyes were soft. Understanding. "Has anyone ever figured out a way to make you shut up?"

Her belly fluttered, and it had nothing to do with Talbott's attack on her. She saw comfort in Mac's gaze, and strength. And an intensity that stirred a response deep inside her. She couldn't look away.

The ambulance stopped beside them, and two paramedics jumped out. One grabbed a pair of bags and the other hurried over to her.

"What happened?" he asked.

"She was attacked. Looks like a knife wound in her side," Mac said, glancing up at the paramedic. A.J. felt abandoned without his eyes on hers, and the feeling frightened her. She struggled to sit up, shrugging Mac's hand off her shoulder.

"I'm fine," she said. "It's just a scratch."

"Ignore her," Mac ordered. "She's in shock."

"I am not in shock!"

The paramedic knelt next to her. "What's your name?" he asked.

"A.J. A. J. Ferguson."

"Tell me what happened, A.J."

"He grabbed me from behind. Around my neck." Her voice wobbled as the horror of the attack washed over her again. "He said he was going to kill me."

"Did he have a knife?"

She frowned, trying to force herself to remember. "I don't know. Maybe. I remember seeing something bright."

The paramedic peeled back the sweater. "It looks like he stabbed you in the side," he said. "We're going to have to take you to St. James."

"No! I don't need to go to the hospital." She heard the panic in her voice and struggled to contain it. "It can't be that bad. Just put a bandage on it."

"We can't do that, A.J. Protocol. Anyone with a knife or gunshot wound has to go to the hospital. At the very least, you need some blood tests."

"Settle down, Ferguson," Mac said. "Just get it over with." A.J. could see the glint of humor in Mac's eyes. "If you behave yourself, I'll go with you to the hospital. I'll even ride in the ambulance with you."

"Now there's a treat I can't resist," she muttered.

Mac laughed and sudden weariness flooded her. She couldn't fight any longer. "Fine. Do what you want."

"My God. Check her for a head injury." Mac's voice, light and teasing, wrapped around her like a warm blanket. She wanted to reach out, to hold onto him for comfort.

She kept her hands to herself.

MAC STOPPED PACING when his partner came through the door of the E.R. waiting room. "Jake. What's going on?"

"Couple things." He handed Mac a purse and a set of keys. "A.J.'s stuff. And I thought you'd want the update. We found a knife and the prints match Talbott's. So it was definitely our buddy who went after A.J."

Anger, barely under control, flared again. "Damn it. I don't suppose patrol found any sign of him."

"Nope. But they're still looking. The captain okayed a stakeout on his house, in case he goes back there."

"He won't."

"Probably not. But who knows? He could have an attack of the stupids." Jake nodded toward the doors that led to the E.R. "How's A.J.?"

Mac scowled. "I have no idea. They won't tell me a damn thing."

"It's just a guess, but I'm thinking you might not have been Mr. Tact when you asked. Let me see what I can find out."

Fear cut into him as he watched Jake smile at the

nurse at the desk. He'd backed down from the steely glitter of her eyes when he'd asked the last time. Because he wasn't sure he wanted to know.

What if A.J.'s injury was worse than he'd thought? What if all the vitality and energy that was A.J. Ferguson was fading away behind those doors?

The depth of his dread rattled him.

His hand closed over the smear of blood drying on his sweater and he tried to rub it away.

The turmoil rolling through him wasn't the cold, merciless anger he felt when a fellow officer was injured in the line of duty. This fury was far more personal.

He wanted his hands on Doak Talbott, wanted to punish him for what he'd done to A.J.

Jake sauntered over, grinning. "She said it's nice to know that some of the detectives in Riverton can be polite."

"We're all proud of you, Mr. Manners. What's going on?"

"A.J.'s just about ready to go. They're releasing her in a few minutes."

Mac tried to ignore the relief that swept through him in a wave. "Great. As long as I'm here, I'll stick around and get her statement," he told Jake, shoving his hands into his pockets.

His partner laughed. "Yeah, you do that, buddy. And make sure you get all the details. It'll probably take a long time. Hours, in fact. Maybe all night."

"What's your problem, Jake? She's one of ours. You want Talbott to get away with this?"

"Whoa, partner." Jake held up his hands. "Take it easy. I'm just jerking your chain."

"The bastard went after Ferguson with a knife. This isn't a joke."

"No," Jake answered, watching him with a thoughtful look in his eyes. "I can see that it isn't."

"Someone from the department needed to be here," Mac said, his voice defensive. He didn't like the speculation in his partner's eyes.

"Absolutely. And who better than you? Your relationship with A.J. has always been so warm and supportive."

"I'm the one who found her. It's my responsibility."

"Yeah," Jake said, nodding. "Absolutely. You're the first one I'd pick."

"You want to make a big deal out of it? Fine. You wait here for her. Be my guest."

Jake laughed and headed toward the door, waving over his shoulder.

Mac scowled at his partner's back. Jake's words had set off alarm bells in his head. The thought of leaving the hospital without seeing for himself that A.J. was okay was unsettling. And disturbing.

Unease slid through him. He'd kept the same vigil for other colleagues. He'd consumed countless cups of undrinkable hospital coffee, paced waiting rooms more times than he'd liked.

But he'd never felt the terror he'd experienced when he saw A.J. lying on the pavement.

And never before had he volunteered to ride in the ambulance with an injured colleague.

It was the situation, he told himself. It was because the perp was Doak Talbott and he wanted the man so badly.

He leaned against the wall and stared at the doors to the E.R. He had to stay. It was his duty.

CHAPTER THREE

"YOU ARE NOT WALKING OUT of this emergency room, Ms. Ferguson." The nurse glared down at her from behind the wheelchair. "If you want to leave, you'll get in this chair. Trust me on that."

"Fine," A.J. muttered. She eased off the table and slid onto the cold vinyl seat. Whatever it took to get out of this hospital.

"Is someone waiting for you?" the nurse asked.

"No. I'll call a taxi."

"Why don't you let me call a friend to pick you up?" the nurse said. Her voice was cheerful and chipper now that she'd gotten her way about the wheelchair. "You'll be more comfortable with someone you know."

She'd also have to wait a lot longer. The smells of antiseptic, blood and medicine clogged her nostrils. She didn't want to think about the last time she'd been in an emergency room, the police, the nurses and doctors staring at her. Pushing away the memories, she said, "I don't want to bother any of them. I just need a taxi."

"Suit yourself," the nurse said as she used her hip to press the disk on the wall that opened the doors. "I'll just park you here while I call."

The nurse wheeled her into place next to the desk, and A.J. gripped the armrests. She wanted to jump from the chair and race out the door.

That would be foolish and weak. And she refused to be weak.

"From that scowl, I assume you're back to normal."

Mac McDougal stood over her, his face tense with worry.

She'd swear it was concern she saw in his eyes. Warmth bloomed inside her but she tried to ignore it.

"McDougal," she said on a sigh. "What are you doing here?"

"I'm just kicking back and relaxing." He cocked his head. "What do you think I'm doing here? I'm waiting for you."

"That wasn't necessary."

"Of course it wasn't." He shrugged and looked away. "But someone had to take your statement."

Disappointment settled over her. "Right." She clenched her hands on the arms of the wheelchair and fought the wave of dizziness sweeping over her. She should have known better than to take the painkiller.

"Can we put this on hold until tomorrow?" she said. "I don't want to deal with it tonight."

"I suppose it can wait." He shoved his hands in his

pockets and didn't quite meet her gaze. "Is someone picking you up?"

"The nurse is calling a taxi for me."

"Forget it. I'll take you home."

Before she could form the words to refuse, he strode over to the nurse and said something in a low voice. Moments later he was back.

"Stay here. I'll get the car." He headed toward the double doors.

"Trudie told me he's been out here the whole time," the nurse said as she watched him leave. "That's so sweet."

A.J. wanted to tell the woman that nothing about Mac McDougal was sweet. He was a complicated man, intense, driven and dominating. No one who knew Mac would use the word *sweet* to describe him.

She didn't bother. The nurse was probably just like all the other women who crossed his path, blinded by the blue of his eyes and the flash of his dimple.

And the power of his body.

A.J. liked being tall, liked that she could look most men in the eye. As much as she hated to admit it, she found big men intimidating. So why did she find Mac's size reassuring?

She shook her head to clear her thoughts as Mac walked in. "I'll take her from here," he told the nurse.

"No, you won't," the nurse replied, stepping in front of him when he tried to take the handles of the chair.

He had a dark SUV idling quietly next to the curb. Mac opened the door and waited for A.J. to get in.

She pulled herself to her feet, then held on to the door as another surge of dizziness swamped her. Closing her eyes, she willed the world to stop twirling around her.

"Hold on," he said. Before she knew what he was doing, he swept her off her feet and onto the seat of the car. Shocked, she stared at him. He'd picked her up as if she weighed no more than a kitten.

Before she could say anything, he slammed the door and got in on the other side. "Need help fastening your seat belt?" he asked.

"No," she said, fumbling for the straps. "I'm fine."

But after she'd tried twice to buckle herself in, he pushed her hands away. "Let me do it."

When he reached across her to grab the seat belt, his arm brushed across her belly, sending out a little flare of heat. He faltered, then yanked on the strapping and shoved the tongue into the slot. His hands covered hers for a moment. They were hard and warm and as tough as Mac. Before she could draw away, he'd retreated to the other side of the SUV.

"You comfortable?" he asked, his voice rough. "That seat belt isn't cutting into anything that hurts, is it?"

"It's fine," she said.

The car jerked as he shifted into gear. "Where do you live?" he asked, clearing his throat.

She gave him her address, then leaned back against the headrest. She'd close her eyes until they were out of the parking lot, she told herself. Just for a minute until she could pull herself together. She felt too raw, too vulnerable to deal with Mac McDougal.

She couldn't face him until all her defenses were firmly in place. Finding Mac waiting for her in the hospital had unnerved her. She needed to regain her composure.

THE HUM SEEMED TO VIBRATE through her body. And it felt like she was flying upward. But she was warm, she thought drowsily. She'd been cold all evening. Now a furnace embraced her.

"Hold on. We're almost there."

Her eyes snapped open. She was in Mac's arms, cradled against his chest, her arms draped around his neck.

Her skin jumped with nerves and her heart raced in her chest. "What are you doing? Put me down."

He grinned down at her. "You don't think I can carry you all the way to your apartment? Forget it, Ferguson. My reputation is at stake here."

They were in the elevator of her apartment building. And she was cuddled up next to Mac like she belonged there. "That's not what I meant."

She struggled to get out of his arms, to stand on her own, but he merely held her more tightly. "Don't you ever accept help, Ferguson? From anyone?"

His words stopped her. "Of course I do. But not from…
from…"

"Not from a colleague?" he asked.

No. Not from you.

She'd accept help gracefully from any of the other
police officers in the department. So why not Mac?

She knew damn well why not.

It was the tension that hummed between them. It
had been there from the beginning, but she'd been
able to suppress it until he bent over her in the parking lot. Until she found him waiting for her in the
hospital.

Until he carried her, sleeping, into the elevator.

Now the tension was out in the open, naked and
pulsing with energy.

Damn the medication. She was too fuzzy-brained to
analyze this. To examine it and explain it away.

"Put me down, Mac."

He ignored her.

The elevator pinged and the doors opened onto her
floor. He strode down the hall, every step jostling her
against his chest.

"Can you stand up while I open the door?" Without
waiting for her to answer, he slid her down his body.
Before she could move away, he put one arm around
her waist, holding her against him while he fumbled
with her keys.

"Where did you get my keys?" she asked, bracing

herself with one hand against the wall. She had a vague recollection of flinging them away from her.

"Jake brought them to the hospital." He looked down at her. "That was smart thinking," he said gruffly. "To push the panic button on your remote. It scared him off."

"No. You stopped him." Alarmed by the dreamy softness in her voice, she put some distance between them.

Distance didn't make any difference. "I got there too late."

"You'll catch Talbott."

Mac held her for another heartbeat, then released her. "Yeah. I struck out on all counts."

She whipped her head around to look at him, but the lock opened with a click. The door to her apartment swung open and the familiar smell wafted out to her, the scent of oranges and cinnamon and fabric softener. When she stumbled through the door, Mac caught her arm. He moved as if to lift her into his arms again, but she stiffened and shifted away from him.

His hand tightened on her arm for a moment, then he released her. "Where's your bedroom?" he asked.

The wound in her side throbbed in time with the pounding in her head. She ached all over and knew she'd be stiff and sore tomorrow. But her stomach jumped at his words.

"I can take it from here, McDougal," she said, putting her hand on the wall and blocking his entry into her apartment. "Thank you for bringing me home."

"I'll stay until you're in bed," he said. "In case you need help."

As if she would ask for his help to change her clothes or assist her into bed. The thought sent a shiver down her spine. "Good line, McDougal. But I'm not biting. Just give me the keys."

There was another pause, and his face was unreadable. "Fine," he said, pressing them into her palm. "I'll see you tomorrow."

He disappeared and she felt deserted. She wanted to call him back. Instead she closed the door and leaned against it.

When she heard the elevator ping, she stumbled into the bathroom. Minutes later she fell into bed and a dark, heavy sleep.

IT WAS THE DARKEST HOUR of the night. Everyone slept, tucked away dreaming in their cozy houses in the cozy town of Riverton.

Everyone but him.

Doak Talbott stood in the shadows and stared at the building on the other side of the street. Rage and hatred thundered in a fierce beat behind his eyes as he studied the house. Floodlights illuminated the grounds, but only one room inside was lit. The rest of the building was dark and silent.

Mindy was a treacherous bitch.

And she was in there. On the other side of that locked door.

He clenched his hands into tight fists as he stared at the house. *She would pay.* Oh yes, she would pay for what she'd done.

She brought the police to his house. And she let them take his son away.

His son.

Was Jamie in there, too?

He had to find the kid.

Sweat rolled down his sides and chilled his skin in the cool evening air. He *had* to have the kid. Jamie had seen too much.

Maybe he'd take care of both problems tonight.

He allowed himself a smile of satisfaction as he stared across the street. She thought she was safe. She thought she could keep him away. Stupid bitch.

She would learn.

She'd beg before he was finished.

He bent down and curled his hand around the cold, greasy handle of the can, then froze. Headlights swung around the corner and a car cruised down the silent street.

He dropped to the ground and crouched behind a tangle of shrubs. The car gradually slowed, then stopped right in front of him.

It was an unmarked police car. Who did they think

they were fooling? A smart man could spot the plain ones every time.

The man in the front seat didn't move. The car continued to hum quietly at the curb as the driver stared out the open window. As if he were watching the place.

Keeping Doak away from Mindy.

Rage boiled up again, dark and consuming. He had to obliterate the barrier between himself and his goal. He would reach through the window and crush the life out of the policeman.

He was halfway off the ground before he managed to control himself. Breathing heavily, blood roaring in his ears, he forced himself back down. He gripped the handle of the can tightly in his fist as he sucked in deep gulps of the night air.

He couldn't afford to lose control. Showing himself to the policeman would be stupid.

And he wasn't a stupid man.

Oh, no. He wasn't stupid at all.

He smiled to himself as he backed away from his hiding place and crept around the corner of the building. There was always tomorrow.

Or the next day.

He glanced over his shoulder at the house one more time before he stepped into the shadows and disappeared.

He would be back.

CHAPTER FOUR

MAC STOPPED HIS CAR in front of the clubhouse but he didn't get out. It was eleven in the morning, and the first wave of golfers was rolling off the course. The bar would be half-full already. His hands tightened on the steering wheel as he watched the steady procession of golf carts unload their passengers at the rear of the building.

The men were relaxed and carefree, laughing and slapping each other on the back. As open and friendly as they seemed, they would instantly close ranks and circle the wagons when an outsider intruded.

He was most definitely an outsider.

He should have let Jake come here. His partner wouldn't have sat in his car, staring at the front door of the Lake View Country Club, measuring the walk up those steps. He'd stroll right in and start asking questions.

But sending Jake would be admitting defeat. It would be admitting that they'd beaten him.

Familiar anger flooded him. *Screw them,* he thought

as he got out of the car. They might have more money than he did, they might be more powerful than a police detective. They'd still answer his questions.

After what Talbott had done to A.J. last night, Mac would make sure these self-important men and women told him everything he wanted to know.

He'd give them no choice.

The door opened with a quiet, dignified whoosh and he stepped inside. The faint, acrid odor of cigar smoke hung in the air, along with the stuffy smells of old leather and older books. A large room lined with book-shelves and filled with leather chairs and couches stood on one side of the hall. A man sat hunched over a computer on the other.

The concierge's eyes widened as he glanced at Mac. "Pierce. What are you doing here?"

Mac pulled out his badge without taking his eyes off the concierge's face, watching for the inevitable reaction.

His face hardened "How can I help you, Officer?"

"It's Detective," Mac said, holding the older man's gaze. "I've moved up in the world."

The man had the grace to flush. "What do you want?"

"Information." Mac nodded his head toward the bar. "I know the way."

"You can't go back there." He half rose from his chair. "That's private property."

Mac continued walking. "I'm aware of that."

The murmur of refined voices and ice clinking against glass drifted out of the bar. Men in golf attire sat around dark tables, reading the newspapers and conversing quietly. There were a few women sprinkled among them, dressed in expensive and discreet clothes. Most of the heads in the room turned to look at him when he walked in.

There was a heartbeat of silence, then the voices began again, a little louder than before. Mac scanned the room, looking for the man he knew would be there. He spotted him sitting at a table, reading the *Wall Street Journal.*

He wove his way through the tables until he reached his target, then sat down in the empty chair.

"Pierce. Good to see you." The man looked across the table with a forced smile and folded the newspaper. "What can I do for you?"

"You can answer a few questions," Mac replied. He leaned back in the chair and crossed his legs comfortably, as if he belonged there.

The man's eyes flickered as he watched Mac. "Certainly," he said in a tight voice, a look of distaste passing over his face.

"Where is Doak Talbott hiding these days?"

Contempt turned the features Mac knew so well to stone. "Doak Talbott isn't 'hiding' anywhere. As far as I know, he's living in the same house he's lived in for years. As you know very well."

"Not anymore, he's not." Mac allowed his fury to show in his eyes. "Maybe you haven't heard. He beat his wife half to death the other night, then started on his kid."

The older man's lips thinned. "I heard someone was spreading stories about him. Mindy always did have hysterical tendencies."

"Hysteria didn't give her two black eyes, a bruise covering half her face and a split lip. Doak did that." Anger pulsed inside Mac like a living thing. "Last night he attacked a member of the police department in our parking lot. We have a positive ID on good old Doak."

Uncertainty filled the older man's eyes for a moment. "I have no idea where Doak might have gone." He looked away and motioned the waitress over. After placing his order, he turned back to Mac. "I'm certain no one else here has heard anything, either."

The waitress backed away, staring hard at Mac and cutting her eyes in the direction of the kitchen.

Understanding the signal, Mac stood. "Excuse me for a moment. I'll be right back."

The back of his neck prickled as he headed for the restroom. No doubt everyone in the room was watching him.

When he rounded the corner, the young woman was waiting for him. "Have you found out where Helena went?" she burst out.

Mac bent closer. "Not yet," he said, in a deliberately

soft voice. "But we're working on finding her. Did you remember something more, Sandy?"

The woman flushed at his use of her name. "No. But all of us are talking about it. Someone might remember something."

"If they do, please call me right away. Even if it doesn't seem important to you." He pulled a card from his wallet and handed it to her.

"I will," she said, staring at the card as if memorizing the information. Then she looked back at him. "Do you think she's all right?"

No. Helena Tripp was dead. He was certain of it. Just as he was certain Doak Talbott was her killer. "I hope so," he said gently. "And the sooner we find her, the happier I'll be."

The waitress pressed her lips together as her eyes brimmed with tears. Nodding, she turned and hurried away.

The people in the room watched him covertly as he made his way back to the table. When Mac sat down, the man across from him asked, "What did the waitress want?"

"The waitress? I went to the restroom."

"She was asking you about that waitress who disappeared, wasn't she?" the older man demanded, scorn in his eyes. "Why are you wasting your time with her? She ran off with a man." Contempt slid across his face. "They all do that. None of them stay here very long."

Why would they? The arrogance and casual contempt permeating this club would destroy your soul if you let it.

"Looking for Helena Tripp is not a waste of my time," he said, using her name deliberately. "She didn't disappear on her own. And this club was the last place she was seen. With Doak Talbott."

"Doak is a good man. He contributes a lot to our community. In fact, he and I are working on a business arrangement that will greatly benefit Riverton."

"And it won't hurt your bottom line either, will it?" Bitter contempt settled in Mac's stomach. "You're doing business with a criminal and a wife beater," he said, making the other man flinch. "I hope you'll get enough money from the deal to wash your conscience clean."

"You shouldn't have come here. I can't help you." The older man's face hardened.

"Then I guess I'll just have to start questioning everyone here at the club about Doak." He glared at the tight-lipped man across the table. "The next time I come here, I'll have subpoenas from a grand jury. I'll haul some asses down to the courthouse, starting with yours. And you can be sure there'll be reporters waiting in the parking lot, cameras running and microphones recording."

"Are you threatening me, Pierce?"

Mac's smile didn't reach his eyes. "I never threaten. I'm just telling you how it's going to be."

A heavy hand dropped onto Mac's shoulder, and he looked up to see a uniformed security guard.

"Let's go, buddy," the guard said. "This is private property."

"Back off, rent-a-cop." Mac flashed his badge. "Even on *private property,* this trumps your tin star."

"It's all right, Randy," the man across the table said. He looked hard at Mac. "The detective is leaving."

Mac stood up. His chair crashed into the table behind it with a dull thud. "Yeah, I've had about as much as I can take of this place." Fury and pain churned in his stomach as he looked at the other man. "But I'll be back. *Dad.*"

A.J. SHIFTED CAREFULLY in her chair again, trying to ease the ache in her back and the throbbing in her side. The woman on the other side of her desk looked at her with concerned eyes. "Are you all right, Ms. Ferguson?"

"I'm fine, Jeanine," A.J. answered with a smile. She forced herself to sit still and relax. She didn't want to shift the focus away from the other woman's problems. "Just a little sore from an accident last night."

"What happened?" Jeanine looked at A.J. fearfully, as if expecting the worst.

"Nothing serious. I took a fall in the parking lot." A.J. smoothed her fingers over the high collar of her silk shirt. She smiled at the other woman with an effort. "I wasn't paying attention."

Before the woman could answer, there was a light

knock on her door. A.J. glanced at her watch. "My next appointment is here, Jeanine. Before you leave, though, let's go over what you're going to say to Todd."

Jeanine twisted her fingers in her lap. "I don't know what to say to him," she whispered.

Jeanine's seventeen-year-old son dominated the household. And he was rapidly spinning out of control. He'd been arrested for fighting two days earlier, the latest in a string of run-ins with the police.

"That's why we talked about rules today," A.J. said. "You're going to set a curfew for him, right?"

"I'll try, but he won't pay any attention to me."

"Then there will be consequences. Right, Jeanine?"

The woman nodded, but A.J. knew she wouldn't follow through. Desperate to find something concrete to help the woman, she said, "Todd has a car, doesn't he?"

Jeanine nodded. "We gave it to him when he turned sixteen."

"Tell him that if he misses his curfew, you'll take his car away."

Jeanine sucked in a breath. "He'll be angry with me."

"Would he hurt you?"

The woman hesitated a second too long. "Todd would never hurt me."

A.J. held Jeanine's gaze, willing some strength and backbone into the woman. "Listen to me. If Todd hurts you, or if you're afraid he'll hurt you, call 911. The police will be at your house in a couple of minutes."

"They'd put him in jail," Jeanine replied, appalled.

"He wouldn't go to jail. He'd go to juvie."

"That's just as bad!"

Memories of antagonistic guards, harshly lit antiseptic-doused hallways and sullen teens flitted through her mind. "Not quite. But I don't want to see him in juvie any more than you do."

"I couldn't do that to him," Jeanine whispered.

"You wouldn't be doing it to him," A.J. replied. "He'd be doing it to himself."

"I couldn't put my baby in jail," she whispered. "I just couldn't. What would happen to him in jail?"

A.J. took a deep, shaky breath, trying to banish the images seared into her brain. "Of course you don't want to do that. What parent would? But Todd has to learn that there are consequences to his actions. He has to learn that he can't do everything he feels like doing. And if the only way he can learn that lesson is a night in juvie, then that's his choice." She stood up and came around to the other side of the desk and crouched in front of Jeanine, taking the woman's hand. "You know it's going to get worse," she said softly. "He's already out of control."

"But jail?" Jeanine breathed.

"I doubt it'll come to that," A.J. said, squeezing the woman's hand. She stood up slowly, feeling every muscle in her body protest. "Teens want discipline. They want to know their parents love them enough to make rules for them. You might be surprised at how Todd responds."

"I'll try," Jeanine said doubtfully. "I'll tell him if he's not home by eleven o'clock, we'll take his car away."

"And then you'll do that, won't you?"

"Yes." Jeanine nodded as she stood up. She straightened and said in a stronger voice, "Yes. I'll take his keys away from him."

"Good for you," A.J. said, putting her arm around the woman's shoulder. "Call me and let me know how you're doing. And come back and talk to me anytime."

"I will, Ms. Ferguson."

"It's A.J., Jeanine. Please call me A.J."

"All right, A.J." The woman gave her a tremulous smile. "Thank you for helping me."

"Remember what we talked about, Jeanine. You're doing this to help Todd."

A.J.'s fingers lingered on her side as she watched the woman threading her way through the desks in the bull pen. She was afraid she'd see Jeanine Jamison again. Todd was an angry young man, and the problems of the Jamison family were complex and difficult. They needed family counseling.

She'd given Jeanine the card of a family counselor. She doubted the woman would even look at it.

"Was Todd Jamison's mother trying to convince you the little punk was just misunderstood?"

Mac's voice came from behind her and she spun

around to face him. One hip rested on his desk and his arms were crossed on his chest. Edginess, frustration and anger swirled around him like a black cloud.

She started to ask him what had happened, what had upset him, but she forced the words back into her mouth. After the unsettling intimacy of the night before, she intended to keep her distance from Mac. "I think Jeanine knows that Todd is in trouble. I think she understands that he needs help."

"I can tell her what Todd needs. And it's not a shoulder to cry on."

A.J. sighed. "He needs discipline and rules. And she's not providing either of them."

"A few nights in juvie might straighten him out."

"That should be our last resort."

Anger simmered in his eyes. "Punks like that only understand one thing. You can only deal with them if they know you're stronger than they are."

"That doesn't make it right," she said in a low voice.

"It makes it smart."

A.J. slid her gaze away from his. As much as she tried to deny it, as much as she wanted to believe otherwise, there was truth in what Mac said.

Sometimes circumstances left you no choice.

People could be pushed only so far. Push them any farther and they shattered.

It was why she tried so hard to help her clients find other ways to cope.

"Might is right?" She raised her eyebrows. "I don't like that vision of society."

"Yeah, well, call me a cynic, but I don't have a lot of faith in the inherent goodness of human nature."

His eyes flickered, and she could swear she saw pain in their depths. Then he pushed himself away from the desk. "And speaking of the goodness of human nature, let's go talk to Doak's wife. Do you think she'll tell us that Doak was misunderstood? That he didn't know what he was doing was wrong?"

Her sympathy for Mac dissolved, leaving the irritation he usually inspired in her. A.J. leaned back into her office to grab her purse, then slammed the door. The echo reverberated through the room. "What crawled up you and died, McDougal?" Brushing past him, she headed for the stairs, not bothering to check that he was behind her. Whatever had stirred between them last night was apparently forgotten. Things were back to normal between them.

Thank goodness.

"Whatever it was, you better unload your attitude before we get to the shelter," she tossed over her shoulder. "You're not going to get much help from Mindy if you approach her like that."

"Don't tell me how to do my job," he snarled. "I know how to talk to witnesses."

But his voice was strained, and she glanced back at him. "What's wrong?" she asked in a softer voice.

He wasn't going to answer. She saw it in the stubborn set of his shoulders and his tightly clenched jaw.

"Mac?" she said. She touched his arm and his muscles tensed and jumped beneath her fingers.

She snatched her hand away.

He looked down at his arm, then met her eyes. "Sorry, A.J. I had a bad interview this morning."

Surprised that he'd told her that much, that he'd apologized, she leaned against the railing, inviting him to talk. "What happened?"

"I was at the country club. I had a run in with my—" He stopped suddenly. "I asked about Doak and didn't get any cooperation," he finally said. He pushed past her on the stairs. "I hope to God Mindy knows something."

She followed him slowly, the rigid set of his shoulders shouting, "keep away." When they reached the door, he held it open and waited for her to walk through.

"I should have asked sooner. How are you feeling today?" he said as they walked across the parking lot. Blinding sunlight hid his expression from her.

"Fine," she said. "A little sore, but I'll survive."

She turned toward her car, but he said, "A little sore, my ass." There was no heat in his words, though. "I'll drive."

In the daylight, his black SUV looked menacing and imposing. *That would be the point,* she thought. Heat rolled out of it in waves when he opened the door. A crushed coffee cup lay on the floor, along with a folded newspaper. He tossed them in the back, then waited for her to climb in.

Her muscles screamed in protest as she pulled herself onto the seat, but she didn't flinch. She didn't want to give him any excuse to touch her.

He climbed inside and studied her. "You didn't take your pain pill this morning, did you?"

"How can that possibly be any of your business?"

He grinned and started the engine, then pulled smoothly into traffic. "You should have taken the pill, Ferguson. You're going to be sore as hell tomorrow."

"There's a news flash," she snapped. "Believe me, I'll be sure not to look for any sympathy from you."

His smile faded as he glanced over at her. "I'm sure you won't. You don't want anything from me, do you?"

Her tiny pause swelled in the hot air. "I want you to catch Doak Talbott," she finally said.

The car accelerated. "That, I can do."

CHAPTER FIVE

FORTY-FIVE MINUTES LATER, drained of energy, A.J. slid onto the seat of Mac's SUV. She would crack if she moved too quickly, splinter and crumble into a million pieces.

"Well, that was sure helpful." Mac slammed his door and shoved the key into the ignition.

"Did you honestly expect Mindy to know where he was?"

Mac sighed. "I expected some ideas, at least. Maybe a place to begin."

"She's a victim of domestic violence." A.J. rested against the seat and drew in a deep, steadying breath. "You know very well that she's easily intimidated."

"Are you telling me I bullied her?"

"No." A.J. looked at his hands resting on the steering wheel and her quick spurt of temper vanished. "You were gentle with her." Surprisingly so. The image of Mac sitting on the floor at Mindy's feet and speaking in a low, calm voice lingered in her mind.

"She still doesn't know squat."

"No. Talbott made sure of that."

Brooding, he tapped the steering wheel. "I need to talk to the kid."

"Jamie? He's only eight years old. I'm not sure he'll be able to tell you much."

"You'd be surprised how much kids know about what's going on in their family."

No, she wouldn't. She knew just how hard families tried to keep secrets, and how readily children saw through the charade.

"He knows far too much," she said quietly. "But how would Jamie know where Doak might have gone?"

"Kids hear a lot more than adults realize."

She knew that, too.

"Shall I call and see if Jamie will talk to you?"

"Yeah." He looked over at her. "And don't say it, Ferguson. I'll take it easy with him."

"I know you will." Avoiding his eyes, she rummaged in her purse for her cell phone. "I take back what I said yesterday."

"You said so many things yesterday. Which nugget of sweetness and light are you retracting?"

She couldn't help the smile that tugged at the corners of her mouth. "The one about bullying your witnesses. You were wonderful with Mindy."

"Not wonderful enough, apparently."

She watched him replay their interview with Mindy, watched him label it a failure. "She didn't have any information to give you."

His sigh held disappointment and frustration. "Yeah. I know that." He glanced over at her and his eyes held cold resolve. "I'm going to find him, A.J. He's going to pay for what he did to you."

"And what he did to Mindy and Jamie; and that poor waitress who disappeared from the country club," she said. She was learning a lot about Mac McDougal, and all of it was surprising. The safe, tidy niche he'd occupied in her mind was crumbling and letting in a flood of disturbing feelings. Feelings she didn't want to examine.

Heat shimmered off the pavement as she called Mindy's sister, Cissy. After a short conversation, A.J. snapped her phone closed and slipped it back into her bag. "She says a visit is fine."

"What time?"

"Right now. Jamie isn't going to school. They can't leave the room." A.J. stared blindly out the window. In her mind's eye she saw Jamie, small and slight, a bruise already blooming on the side of his face. His blond hair was matted with sweat and he cowered in the corner of the Talbott's living room, his gaze locked on his mother. Mindy sat on a couch, holding a bloody towel to her face, ignoring the fluttering neighbor who'd called the police. Mindy's eyes held the blank and hopeless expression A.J. had seen too often in victims of domestic violence.

The shock, fear and confusion in Jamie's eyes would haunt her for a long time.

"Damn Doak Talbott to the deepest corner of hell."

A muscle twitched in Mac's jaw and his hands tightened on the steering wheel. "Where are the kid and his aunt staying?"

"DCFS put them in the Tarrington Hotel under fake names."

In a few minutes they stood in the hall, knocking on the door to a suite. A maid pushing a heavy cart gave them a curious glance.

The door opened and a younger, more vibrant version of Mindy stood in front of them. "Ms. Ferguson?"

"Yes, and this is Detective McDougal," she answered. "Are you sure Jamie is up to answering a few questions?"

Cissy sighed. "Frankly, I don't know. He hasn't said much of anything to me. I'm worried about him."

"I'll see if a therapist who specializes in children can come over to the hotel," A.J. said. "Jamie needs to talk to someone."

"Good." Cissy looked at her and Mac helplessly. "I don't know what to say to him, what to do. He just sits on the floor, playing with his cars or his Transformers. He barely looks at me when I talk to him. He's breaking my heart."

"You're doing exactly what needs to be done," Mac said. He took her arm and steered her toward the other side of the room, away from Jamie. "You're someone he knows, someone he feels comfortable with, and you're keeping him safe."

Mac eased her into a chair at the tiny table and took

her hands in his. Cissy stared into his eyes, her entire attention focused on him.

The legendary McDougal charm strikes again.

The snake of jealousy that slithered through A.J. both shocked and alarmed her. Mac was doing his job. And even if he wasn't, even if he was merely flirting with Cissy Gregory, she had no reason to be jealous of Mac's attention to another woman.

No *right* to be jealous.

Her head ached and her chest burned as she turned away from the sight of Mac's dark head bent close to Cissy's blond one. Jamie was what mattered here, she reminded herself sharply. Only Jamie.

Trying to compose herself, she watched Mac approach. "Let me talk to Jamie," he said in a low voice. "You deal with Cissy. Emphasize the rules. No leaving the hotel room, no phone calls and make sure she understands how important that is. Make sure she doesn't do anything that would make it easy for Doak to find them."

Without waiting for her answer, he approached Jamie, stopping several feet away. He sat on the floor easily, tucking his long legs in front of him. She watched for a heartbeat then took a deep breath and turned to Cissy, pasting a smile onto her face.

Mac heard the quiet murmur of A.J.'s voice behind him as he eased to the floor. Immediately the boy scooted away until his back hit the couch. Unable to go any farther, he stared at Mac fearfully.

Mac's heart twisted in his chest. Instead of moving closer, he settled back and waited.

When he made no effort to approach Jamie, the boy straightened with a confused look.

Mac tried to make himself as unthreatening as possible. Finally the boy stirred.

"You were at our house when…" He touched the bruise on the side of his face.

"Yeah, I was there." Mac nodded approvingly. "You're a smart boy, Jamie. You notice things."

Jamie's nod was jerky. "I remember you."

Mac smiled and forced himself to relax. "How are you feeling, kid?"

Jamie touched his face again. "I want my mom."

"I know you do," Mac answered softly. "But your mom is in a special house right now. People are taking care of her, and she needs to be by herself."

His face paled. "Is she going to die?"

"She's not going to die, Jamie. She's got a bruise on her face, just like you. In fact, you're the bruise twins. She has a cut lip, too. But she's getting better."

Jamie bowed his head and tears glistened on his eyelashes. "I want her. I'll be good. I promise."

Rage at Doak Talbott exploded through him, roaring through his veins and pounding in his head. Mac closed his eyes, struggling to control it. Anger would only frighten Jamie more.

"I saw your mom today, and she wants you, too. She

told me what a great kid you are." Mac leaned forward, encouraged when Jamie didn't flinch away. "What happened isn't your fault, Jamie. It's not your mom's fault, either. It was your dad's fault. He did a bad thing."

"Where is my dad?" Jamie asked in a small voice.

"I don't know. He ran away." Mac leaned closer. "He ran away because he knew he did a bad thing. He knew it was his fault, not yours and not your mom's."

"He said I had to go away with him." Jamie's mouth quivered with fear.

"No, you don't. We won't let him take you. You're going to stay with your aunt until your mom is feeling better. All right?"

Jamie picked up two pieces of a Transformer and shoved them blindly together, but he couldn't make them fit. "He said it was all my mom's fault. He said she made him angry. He said he would kill us."

"Nobody's going to hurt you, Jamie. Or your mom. We're going to find your dad and make sure he can't hurt you ever again. Okay?" Mac took the pieces of the toy and snapped them together, then laid it on the floor.

Jamie took the toy and examined it.

"You could help us find him," Mac said.

Jamie looked up, caution in his eyes. "How?"

"Smart kids like you hear lots of things. And they re-member things, too." Mac picked up another two pieces and snapped them together. "Did your dad ever get mad at you because you heard something he said? Did he ever do something then tell you not to say anything?"

Panic blossomed on Jamie's face, and he shook his head so hard the toy fell to the floor. "No!"

"Did your dad say he'd hurt you if you told?" Mac made his voice as gentle as he could.

Jamie stared at the carpet and a tear rolled down his face.

"I won't let him hurt you, Jamie. I promise. Your dad isn't going to hurt you or your mom, ever again." He kept his eyes fixed on the top of Jamie's head as he fitted together another piece. "Do you know about good secrets and bad secrets?"

The boy used his toe to nudge the Transformer and didn't answer.

"This is a bad secret, Jamie. This is the kind of secret you're supposed to tell an adult."

"I didn't hear him say anything," Jamie finally said, picking up the toy and clutching it to his chest. His voice was so low that Mac could barely hear him.

"Did he ever say anything about going away?"

"Yes." He looked at Mac out of fear-drenched eyes. "He said Mom would go away to hell. And she'd take me with her."

Mac wanted to enfold the child in his arms and promise him he was safe. He wanted to protect him from the evil in his world, the evil that was his own father.

A tear slid down Jamie's face and dripped off his nose. Mac clenched his fists, then relaxed them. He touched the boy on the knee as he rose to a crouch in front of him. "If you think of anything you need to tell me, I want you to call me. Can you do that, Jamie?"

The boy gave an almost imperceptible nod.

Mac pulled a business card out of his pocket. "Here's my phone number," he said, giving the card to Jamie. "All you have to do is call me and I'll be here." He knew Jamie didn't understand about business cards, but he hoped like hell the small white rectangle would give the kid a little sense of security.

Jamie studied the card, then looked up at Mac. "My dad's real big," he whispered.

"I'm bigger," Mac answered. "You want to stand up and see for yourself?"

Jamie hesitated, then he scrambled to his feet, still holding the toy and the business card. He aligned himself next to Mac, leg to leg, then looked up at him, his eyes measuring.

"What do you think?" Mac asked.

Jamie nodded slowly and his eyes brightened. "You *are* bigger than my dad. You could beat him up."

"I sure could." And given the slightest excuse, he'd beat the hell out of Doak.

Jamie stepped away but he didn't take his eyes off Mac. "My dad…" he began, then his aunt came up and wrapped her arm around him.

"Your favorite show is on, honey. Do you want to watch it?"

Jamie nodded and the moment was gone. Cissy led him into one of the bedrooms, and the television clicked on. The sounds of *Sesame Street* drifted out of the room.

Moments later Cissy came back, pulling the door to the room partially closed behind her. "He doesn't like to miss *Sesame Street*," she said. "I try to make sure he sees it every day." She wrapped her arms around herself. "It's one small constant I can give him."

Mac controlled the frustration welling up inside him. Jamie had been about to reveal something to him, something that could be important. But Cissy was right. Familiar routines were all the kid had to hold on to right now.

"I understand. Jamie's lucky to have you," he said gruffly. "But if he says anything more, or remembers anything, please call me right away. Night or day." He touched her arm. "I'm here to help you and so is A.J."

She took the card he gave her and studied it, then looked up at him. "I'll do that, Mac."

"If you need anything, anything at all, call us."

Cissy slipped his card into her pocket and her face hardened. "The only thing I need is for you to catch that monster before he completely destroys Mindy and Jamie."

"I'm working on it, Ms. Gregory, and so are a lot of other police officers. We'll find him."

He looked over at A.J., who was standing near the door. She stood next to the wall, holding herself stiffly upright. Her knuckles were white on the doorknob.

The stubborn woman was too proud to admit she hurt. Worry about Jamie and his aunt faded as he watched A.J. He wanted to ease her in to a chair, to make sure she was comfortable. He wanted to do a hell of a lot more than make her comfortable.

He motioned for her to open the door. "Let's go, Ferguson."

She turned to Cissy. "Please call me anytime you have questions or just need to talk. And get in touch with the therapist. Jamie needs to see someone."

"I will. Thank you for coming by." She gave them a weary smile.

"Any time," Mac said.

He pulled the door closed behind them and steered A.J. toward the elevator. When he noticed her walking stiffly beside him, he steadied her with a hand on her elbow.

She leaned into him for a moment. "Was Jamie able to give you any information?"

"Not a thing, other than to confirm that Doak is a dirt bag of the first degree."

He wanted to touch A.J. again. Instead, he shoved his hands in his pockets. "He almost said something right before Cissy interrupted him."

The elevator arrived and they got inside. The air

smelled vaguely of cigarette smoke and air freshener, and the carpet needed to be vacuumed.

"At least he was talking to you. That's frankly more than I expected."

"I'll talk to him again. See if I can get him to trust me."

"Good luck," she said under her breath.

He rounded on her. "Are you saying that I didn't handle him right? What would you have done differently?"

"You handled him perfectly," she said. "You said exactly what he needed to hear."

"Then sooner or later he'll trust me."

"No, he won't." A shadow passed over her face. "It's very hard for abused children to trust. It takes a long time." She looked up at him, her eyes unreadable again. "We don't have a long time to find Doak."

He wanted to ask her about the sadness in her face, about the pain in her eyes. He wanted to know more about A. J. Ferguson. He wanted to know what made her tick, what she thought and who she was.

He wanted to know if she tasted as complicated and seductive as she looked.

He wanted to know if the passion she brought to her job spilled over into the rest of her life.

Hell, he wanted her, period.

Having her was another story.

One that didn't have a happy ending.

CHAPTER SIX

CLOUDS SCUDDED across the night sky, hiding the moon, and the streetlight on the corner provided only a thin slice of illumination. Shadows shrouded the house across the street, the windows and doors an indistinct blur.

Darkness was good. Unlike the weak fools who were afraid of the night, he embraced it. He was powerful enough, and strong enough, to work with it.

Heavy with humidity, the still air held heat from the day. It pressed down on him as he waited. He could be patient. He'd watched the house for two nights now. He knew the single light in the first floor room would soon go out. Another light would shine briefly in an upstairs window, then that light, too, would wink out. The house would settle into sleep.

He could wait.

No lights shone in any of the other boring houses on the dreary, boring block. And no cars had ventured down the street for the past half hour.

A few dried leaves rustled beneath the bushes. The

vinyl siding of the house where he waited was cool against his back. He pulled the red can closer, smiling at the sound of the liquid sloshing inside. Yes, he could wait.

A half hour after the last light was extinguished, he struggled to his feet. His blood tingled with anticipation and his muscles flexed and bunched. He was ready.

No cars.

No signs of life.

Good. There would be no surprises.

Taking a deep breath, fighting the excitement building inside him, he grabbed the can and hurried across the street. He'd have to work fast. The landscaping didn't offer any places to hide. Mounds of impatiens lined the front and sides of the house, the flowers too low to conceal anything bigger than a rabbit.

He stepped into the mass of blooms, ignoring the sweet scent that drifted up from beneath his shoes. The can opened with a rusty groan and the pungent smell of gasoline blotted out any trace of the flowers.

As he splashed the gasoline along the wooden siding of the house, it ran toward the ground in dark, wet smears. A few drops splashed onto his Cole Haan loafers. He was almost at the corner of the building before the can was empty.

He tossed the can to the ground behind him, and it landed with a dull clank. Then, leaning toward the house, he lit a match and tried to throw it against the siding.

The match flared and blew out immediately. He lit another, then another.

They all blew out before leaving his hand.

Swearing viciously, he struck another match and cupped his hand around it. Before he reached the dark, wet spot of gasoline, vapors ignited with a whoosh. Flames leaped out at him, curling around his hand and licking at his face and feet. He dropped the match and stumbled back, cursing and shaking his singed hand. The sickly sweet smell of burned hair swirled around him. He swiped frantically at his face, brushing away sparks of pain.

Flames erupted with a roar and he flung up his hands as he stumbled away from the house. Searing heat punched at him and he staggered toward the street, stooping to grab the empty gas can. Greedy fingers of fire spread over the siding. The paint blistered and peeled away, and the wood crackled as it turned black. Plumes of oily black smoke mushroomed in the air and slithered through open windows into the house. He stood and watched the fire until the increasing heat forced him back.

The side of the house was engulfed in flames by the time he made his way to his hiding place across the street. Crouching in the bushes again, he imagined Mindy waking up to the heat and smoke of the fire, imagined her panicking as she tried to make her way out of the house.

The bitch deserved to die.

His son would die, too.

A picture of Jamie ran through his mind, but he pushed it away. Jamie had left him no choice.

The piercing screech of an alarm tore through the quiet of the night, its steady wailing assaulting his ears. A few moments later the front door of the house across from him crashed open and a flood of women in nightgowns and pajamas crowded out the door.

The wail of sirens in the distance cut through the women's frightened voices. The women surged toward him, away from the house, and Doak crouched lower.

They stopped in the street, huddling close together, staring at the burning house with dazed and bewildered eyes. In spite of the heat from the fire, many of them wrapped their arms around their chests, as if they were cold. They hadn't seen him, he realized with a rush of relief. His eyes darted from one face to another, looking for Mindy and Jamie. He thought he saw Mindy, then she turned her back.

It couldn't have been Mindy, he decided as he studied the worn robe the woman wore. Why would Mindy wear trash like that? She had a closet full of designer clothes.

Flashing lights bounced off the window across the street and colored the scene in front of him. One fire engine rolled around the corner and stopped. A fire truck and another engine followed. Firefighters flung open the doors and rushed out almost before it had parked. Their barked orders mingled with the sobs of the women and the roar of the flames to push a wall of sound at him.

The firefighters wove through the crowd, hauling thick coils of hose behind them. He couldn't see any faces now as the women all turned to watch the water battle the flames. It was impossible to tell if Mindy or Jamie was among them. Two firefighters rushed through the front door, the apparatus over their faces making them look like a pair of giant insects.

He ached to wait, to see them carry Mindy's lifeless body out the door, but he didn't dare. Two police cars pulled up behind the fire engines, and judging by the sirens in the distance, more were on their way.

It was time to leave, to fade into the crowd of neighbors gathering to watch the fire and disappear. He wasn't going to be one of those stupid people who lingered at a fire and was caught. He was much smarter than that.

With one last look at the smoldering house, he turned and crept through the bushes framing his hiding place. He emerged at the edge of the property and glanced down at the gasoline can he still carried. He tossed it into the dark cavern beneath the front porch of the next house, then walked down the driveway, as if he'd cut over from the next block to see the excitement. Nodding to the people standing on the sidewalk, he slipped his hands into his pockets and casually walked away.

As A.J. DREAMED, knocking changed into the sound of a fist hitting something solid. A.J. turned uneasily in her sleep as she ran through her apartment in her dream. A man stood in the kitchen, his face contorted in anger, repeatedly slamming his fist against a wall. The crack of his hand hitting the wall drowned out his voice. She had no idea what he was saying.

The pounding stopped abruptly, and she shot up in bed. Her heart raced in her chest and a sob caught in her throat. Remnants of the dream clung to her like cobwebs, and she struggled to banish it. Sweat filmed her chest and legs and, suddenly shivering, she wrapped her arms around herself.

"A.J.! Answer the door!"

Mac's voice. Outside her apartment. The doorknob rattled as he shook it, and she stumbled out of bed. Disoriented, trying to sort out reality from the lingering fragments of the dream, she hurried toward the door.

"What?" She braced herself against the wall and took a deep breath.

"It's Mac. Open the damn door."

She flipped the dead bolt and tugged at the door. It opened only a few inches, held in place by the chain.

Mac pulled the door closed and said, "Take off the chain."

Slippery with sweat, her fingers fumbled with the tiny knob at the end of the chain. Finally she managed to unhook it. Pulling the door open, she squinted against the light pouring in from the hall. "What's going on? What are you doing here?"

He pushed the door open wider and she stepped aside to let him in. His eyes darted from one side of the living room to the other, checking and cataloging.

Finally he looked at her. "Are you all right?"

"I'm fine." She frowned, still foggy with sleep. "Does it look like there's anything wrong with me?"

His gaze swept over her, more slowly than necessary. Cool air from the open door swept over her bare legs and puckered her nipples beneath the thin T-shirt she wore to bed. His gaze lingered on the boxers she used as pajama bottoms.

A ripple of awareness washed over her. Her face heated and she raised her chin. "Seen enough, McDougal?"

He lifted his gaze to her face. In the light from the hall his eyes were hot and dark. "Oh, yeah, Ferguson." He moved closer and touched her face, trailed a finger down her cheek. As it drifted lower, he froze. Then he skimmed a knuckle over a bruise on her neck before dropping his hand.

Her stomach jumped and she resisted the impulse to cross her arms over her chest. "What are you doing here?" she whispered.

"You don't think this is a social visit?" He tried to smile but his face was grim.

In spite of the shadows playing across his face, she

could see the strain in his eyes and lines of weariness bracketing his mouth. His hair stood up, as if he'd run his hands through it once too often.

"What's wrong, Mac?" she asked. She reached out and touched his hand, then drew back too quickly.

His gaze dropped to her hand, lingered there for a moment. Then he lifted his head, met her eyes. His were carefully blank.

"Sit down," he said quietly.

She curled up in a corner of the couch, as far away from him as she could get. He threw himself into a chair across from her and scrubbed a hand across his face. "There was a fire at the women's shelter Mindy was staying at tonight. Someone doused a wall with gasoline."

Horror clogged her throat. She leaned toward him, her self-consciousness forgotten. "Was anyone hurt? How bad was the damage?"

"No one's hurt. Everyone got out in time, thanks to smoke detectors. The fire department got there right away and put out the fire before it burned through the wall. But there was enough smoke and water damage that the women will have to stay somewhere else for a while."

"Who would do such a thing?" she whispered. "Setting fire to a house full of women and children."

"Doak Talbott, for one. And a lot of the other scumbags who put women in that shelter." His voice was hard and implacable. "We're going to track every one of them down and check their alibi for last night."

She gazed at Mac for a moment, the pieces falling into place. Something danced in her stomach. He'd come here to check on her.

He looked too large for her tiny living room, too full of vitality to be confined within its walls. His black T-shirt highlighted the muscles in his chest and his powerful arms. The faded, worn denim of his jeans clung to his legs, hard muscles sheathed by soft fabric.

Her hands tightened on the couch cushion. "Did you come here tonight to make sure Doak hadn't found me?"

"He already attacked you once. If he's behind that fire, I have to figure you're next on his list." He held her eyes for a moment, then his gaze dropped down.

"Thank you for checking on me," she said, shifting her legs beneath her. Warmth spread where his gaze touched her. "I appreciate it, Mac. But since you can see that I'm fine, I'll let you get going." She studied his tired eyes for a moment, trying to ignore her body's signals. "You look like you need some sleep."

A weary grin briefly lit his face. "Don't you know there's no rest for the wicked, Ferguson?"

"If that's true, Doak will never sleep again."

Mac's grin vanished. "No one sleeps in hell."

The memory of Doak's hands on her neck blended with the lingering uneasiness from her dream. She touched her side, felt the bandage beneath her shirt, and she wanted to reach out for comfort. For Mac.

Time to end this.

She stood. "Thanks for letting me know, Mac." She headed for the door, but he stopped her with a touch.

Tiny shock waves rippled through her, and she looked down at his fingers on her skin. *Move away,* she told herself.

"I didn't come here just to warn you." His voice was low and raspy, as if his throat had suddenly closed. "I came to protect you. I'm going to stay here tonight in case Doak shows up."

Her stomach jumped and she stood there, frozen by the naked need in his eyes and her own response. When she swallowed, his gaze dropped to her throat.

"That's not necessary," she said. "He doesn't know where I live."

"Are you sure, A.J.? Sure enough to bet your life on it?" He leaned in, and she smelled coffee on his breath. "Nobody's supposed to know where the women's shelter is. But someone found it. My money's on Doak."

His hand tightened on her arm and his fingers slipped down to her wrist. Nerves popped beneath her skin and wildness raced through her blood.

They stood facing each other, close enough for her to feel the heat radiating from him, close enough she was afraid he'd hear the pounding of her heart.

"It doesn't matter what I believe," she whispered.

"You're not my personal bodyguard. I can take care of myself." But her treacherous body hungered to feel Mac's arms around her, to revel in his strength and know she could lean on him.

Understanding filled his eyes. "You always have, haven't you, A.J.?" He brushed her hair away from her cheek. "Even when you were hurt you didn't want any help. But it's okay to take once in a while."

"It looks like you're the one who needs help tonight," she said. "You haven't slept, have you? You're exhausted." She reached up, needing to soothe away the fatigue, the pain. Her hand curved around his cheek, the bristles of his beard rubbing against her fingers, her thumb smoothing the lines of weariness.

His hand covered hers, pressing her palm against his cheek. "Maybe we need each other tonight."

She eased her hand away from him. "No, Mac. I can't give you what you want."

"I only want as much as you're willing to give."

She longed to take that final step toward him, to take what he offered. But instead she broke contact with him. It felt like she'd ripped off a limb.

"I don't have anything to give you," she said, curling her fingers into her palm. "You've already done too much."

"You think this was a hardship for me?" His mouth curved into a smile. "That I had to force myself to come here tonight?"

"I can't get involved with you, Mac."

"Because we work together?"

If only that were the reason. Longing tore at her heart and regret filled her mouth with the bitter taste of her past. She pressed her lips together before she could blurt out the truth.

"Isn't that enough?" she said instead.

"I used to think so. Now I'm not sure. I can't get you out of my head, A.J."

"It wouldn't work." Her fingers touched the place on her wrist where he'd held her. "You know nothing about me."

"That's easily remedied."

"I don't hop into bed with every man I'm attracted to."

His eyes darkened. "I'm glad to know this…attraction goes both ways."

"I didn't say that."

"You don't have to." He picked up her hand and slid two fingers over her wrist. "I can feel your pulse jump when I touch you."

She tugged her hand way, but not before her heart stuttered and began to race.

"Besides, I'm not saying you have to jump into bed with me." His eyes crinkled into a grin again and his dimple flashed. "Although I wouldn't say no if you asked."

"I'm not asking," she said, her voice catching in her throat.

"I'm devastated, but I'll try to struggle through it." He gave her another smile, the kind that made her knees weaken and her stomach flutter.

She stepped away from him, away from temptation. "Thank you for coming by," she said, clearing her throat. Her voice sounded foreign, low and smoky and seductive. "I'll see you at work tomorrow."

He shoved his hands in his pockets and leaned against the wall as he studied her. She couldn't look away.

What would it feel like to have Mac's arms around her, to be cradled against his broad shoulders? What would his long, muscled legs feel like against hers? The pressure points at the juncture of his legs where the denim had worn white gleamed in the dim light. He gave her a half-grin. "You're tough, Ferguson, I'll give you that. But I've always liked a challenge."

He pushed away from the wall. "Now, about tonight. I'll leave if you want me to, but I'm not going anywhere. I'll spend the night on the floor outside your door." His half-grin widened. "Think of what your neighbors will say in the morning."

Humiliation swept through her as she pictured the avid curiosity on her neighbors' faces. "You'd do it, wouldn't you?" she muttered. "I'm tempted to call your bluff. I'd love to see you sleeping on the floor in the hall." But she was already going to the linen closet. Removing sheets, blankets and a pillow, she tossed them in his direction.

"You can have the couch."

"A.J.?"

His voice stopped her, and she turned to face him. "What?"

"Don't bother to lock the door. It wouldn't slow me down for more than five or ten seconds. And if something comes up, I'll need to get to you in a hurry."

His lips twitched as he watched her, and her pulse jumped again. She flattened her palms against the closet door. "Let's be clear on this, McDougal. If you come into my bedroom, there better be blood or fire in my living room."

"Got it, ma'am." He gave her a mock salute and disappeared into the living room.

"Oh, yeah," he said from around the corner. "I do love a challenge."

CHAPTER SEVEN

A.J. SLID BACK TO SLEEP and into the dream. This time the man was behind her as she ran down the hall. He swung a thick leather strap that whistled through the air and cracked against the wall with a sharp slap.

There was a woman in the kitchen who kept her face carefully turned as she peeled potatoes for dinner.

A.J.—a child now—dashed into her bedroom and pushed into the closet, cowering behind the starched dresses and the school uniform. When she stumbled over her patent-leather Mary Janes, she kicked them aside. A box tumbled from a shelf and paper dolls spilled onto the floor.

"Angelina. Do you think you can hide from me?"

He spoke softly, almost gently as he bounced the strap off his hand. A.J. scooted away until she was pressed into the corner.

"No!" she cried. "No!"

A.J. shot up in bed, her chest heaving, her heart racing with panic. Clutching the sheet, she scanned the room frantically.

No one was in her bedroom.

She was in her apartment. Alone.

She took a shuddering breath, then another. The light from her alarm clock glowed a soft green, telling her it was 2:37 a.m. The familiar shapes of her furniture, her pictures on the wall, the chair next to the window reassured her.

Soothed her.

But she wouldn't sleep again tonight.

She slipped out of bed and opened her bedroom door. The pale glow of the moon seeped into the living room, painting the outlines of her blinds on the wall. She headed toward the couch, toward the book she'd been reading, then jerked to a stop.

Mac.

The dream had driven him from her mind.

He'd come to protect her, to keep her safe. And as she watched him sleeping on the couch, the horror of the dream receded.

His big body was sprawled over the cushions, one arm hanging to the floor. He lay on his stomach, the sheet twisted around his waist. She could see only a pale sliver of his face in the dim light. His feet hung over the end of the couch, uncovered, and she wanted to pull the blanket over them.

He'd take up a lot of space in a bed, she thought as she watched the rise and fall of his broad, smooth back. What would it be like to share a bed with him? Would

he wrap his arms around his lover while they slept, pull
her tight against him in the night?

Would he rise over her in the dawn light, press his
mouth to hers, fuse their bodies together?

She let her gaze slide over him, from the dark hair
curling at his neck, to the muscles of his back beneath
the taut T-shirt, to the curve of his buttocks beneath the
blanket. His legs looked impossibly long in the darkness, and she imagined them twined around her own
legs.

Her heart thudded against her chest, the slow, heavy
beats matching the throbbing lower down in her body.

A.J. backed out of the living room. She was invad-
ing Mac's privacy when he was most vulnerable.
Watching him sleep was an intimate act, one that lovers shared.

She had no right to watch him.

The kitchen linoleum was cold against her feet, a
welcome jolt. Heat still bubbled up inside her, and she
braced her hand on the counter, willing it away.

The faint scent of coffee, the subtle, sweet aroma of
fruit and spices that filled the kitchen, brought the
dream creeping back.

Anxiety swept through her, and unnerving remnants
of the dream returned. Telling herself to snap out of it,
she wrapped her arms around her chest.

Something touched her shoulder and she recoiled,
her hand instinctively closing over the handle of a knife

in the block on the counter. She whirled around in a crouch, extending the blade in front of her.

"Whoa!" Mac held up his hands and took a step backward. "It's me."

She blinked, staring at his rumpled hair, his jeans unbuttoned at the waist, his wrinkled T-shirt. She dropped her hand. Cool steel brushed against her leg, and she looked down at her side. When she saw the knife, her hand began to tremble.

His eyes locked with hers, Mac slowly reached for her hand, lifted her wrist. He pried her fingers away from the handle and set the knife on the counter.

"What's wrong?" he asked quietly.

"I didn't hear you come up behind me," she said, lacing her hands behind her back, trying to banish the feel of the knife, the instinctive fear that had swept through her.

"So you pulled a knife on me?" He watched her steadily but didn't try to touch her.

"You startled me."

"Most people jump when they're startled, or they swear." His eyes were alert with questions. "They don't pull a knife and go into a crouch."

"I'm not most people." She turned her back to him.

She heard his bare feet on the linoleum, felt him move closer. "What's going on, A.J.?"

She swallowed, searching for an answer that would satisfy him. "My side," she blurted. "It hurts. I was going to change the bandage. That's why I had the knife."

His hands settled on her shoulders, then slid down her arms. "That's quite a knife for a bandage."

"I couldn't find my scissors in the dark. I didn't want to turn the light on and wake you up."

Gently he turned her so she faced him. "That was thoughtful of you," he whispered. His face was shadowed and his eyes dark. "You should have said something in the living room. I would have helped you."

"You were awake?" Appalled, she tried to draw her hands away from him. But he held on.

"I was awake. I waited for you to come closer. I wanted you to come to me."

"I—I—" she stuttered.

"It's okay," he murmured. Slowly he brought his hands up and cupped them around her face. He brushed his thumbs over her lips, tracing their shape, lingering in the corners of her mouth. "It's okay, A.J."

Still holding her face between his hands, he bent close enough for her to taste his breath. Then, his lips hovering above hers, he slid his thumb between them. The callused pad glided over her mouth, pressed lightly. Her stomach swooped at the sensation and her lips parted.

His mouth replaced his thumb, and he slid his tongue along the seam between her lips. Heat surged through her and she moved closer, until their bodies met from chest to legs.

For a moment she lost herself in him, in the need driving through her. Mac's hands roamed over her possessively, wrapping around her, pulling her tight against him.

He touched the cut on her side and she couldn't suppress the involuntary flinch. He froze, then pulled his mouth away from hers. He rested his forehead against hers for a moment. Finally, drawing a deep, unsteady breath, he lifted his head.

"I need to take a look at your side," he said, his voice hoarse. "Now. While I can still think."

She wanted to tell him that she'd been lying, that there was nothing wrong with her side. She wanted to pull him against her, to feel his legs twined with hers, his body imprinted onto hers.

She wanted him.

She held onto him for another moment, then slowly let him go. Nodded. "The scissors are in that drawer," she said, her voice shaky.

He kept one arm around her, while he reached into the drawer. A moment later he laid the scissors on the counter.

Taking a step back, he slid his hand down her side, brushing her breast. Her breath hitched and her knees weakened.

He looked down at her T-shirt, at the faded, almost illegible logo across her breasts. He rubbed the worn material between his fingers. "One of your favorites?"

She nodded. "A…friend gave it to me."

He crushed the material in his fist. Then he smoothed it out, his hand splaying on her belly. Her muscles quivered beneath the heat of his palm.

"I'll be careful with it," he said.

He folded the hem up, over and over, until the T-shirt was bunched above her waist. The square of gauze that covered her wound stood out, stark white against her skin. For a moment he stared at her exposed abdomen.

Then he skimmed a finger down her belly, paused at the waistband of her shorts. Slowly he eased the finger beneath the elastic, tugged it so that it snapped against her side.

She sucked in a breath as heat pooled between her legs.

"Nice boxers. Who left them behind?" His eyes met hers. "The same guy who gave you the T-shirt?" He swept his hand down her hip, brushed over the swell of her cheek, trailed down her leg.

"No one," she managed to say. "No one left them behind."

Mac studied A.J. in the shadows of the kitchen, watching her eyes go soft and unfocused as he touched her. Her long, slim body vibrated beneath his hands. She wanted him. Her mouth had trembled beneath his. Her pulse had jumped when he pressed his lips to her throat.

Mac let his hand linger on the boxers. He wanted to

rip them away, to savor the sweet curves beneath them. He wanted to fill his hands with her, to touch her everywhere. "I'm glad," he said, his voice barely a murmur in the darkness. "I'm glad there's no one with a claim on you."

Need flared in her face. She wanted him as much as he wanted her. He could press her against the counter, surround her, and she wouldn't resist. He could have her tonight.

It would be a mistake.

He didn't want a one-night stand from A.J., he realized with a ripple of shock as he clutched her hips more tightly, then deliberately relaxed his grip.

They could make love tonight. It would take only a touch, a kiss and she would come to him. But tomorrow she'd look at him with the aloof eyes she showed the rest of the world. Tomorrow she'd regret her weakness, regret her desire. And she wouldn't allow herself to need again.

If they made love tonight, she'd close herself off from him. He'd never get the answers he suddenly craved.

So instead of pulling her closer, he picked up the scissors with hands that shook. "Let's get a look at those stitches."

Before he could cut away the bandage, she laid her hand on his. "Don't worry about it, Mac," she said. "It's feeling much better. I guess I needed to move around."

He turned his palm to hers, laced their fingers together. "What woke you up, A.J.? Why did you come out here? It wasn't the stitches."

A shadow of pain, of fear flooded her eyes, then was gone. She shrugged. "A bad dream," she finally muttered.

"Want to talk about it?"

"No." Her voice trembled. "It was nothing. I've already forgotten it."

He pulled her against him again and her arms snaked around him, held on. He wondered if she realized the desperation in her grip.

She didn't want to go to sleep.

Didn't want to dream.

He closed his eyes. Her hair smelled of oranges and the faint, distinctive scent he associated with her. "A.J.," he murmured into her ear, "let's get you to bed."

He heard her breath hitch, a tiny sound in the back of her throat. "Yes," she whispered. Her hands trembled against his back and his body tensed with need.

He leaned back, pushing the dark cloud of her hair away from her face. "A.J., I don't think I've ever wanted anything as much as I want to get in that bed with you. But that's not what you need."

She managed an unsteady smile. "Don't you think I should be the judge of that?"

He brushed his lips across her forehead. "I don't want to be a warm body that keeps your nightmares away. I want to be the man you make love with."

He felt the heat rising in her cheeks and she pushed herself away from him. "Say what you think, Mac. Don't hold back." Humiliation at his refusal swam in her eyes.

"Hey, give me a little credit," he said, keeping his voice light. "I'm trying to do the right thing here. I'm being noble, sacrificing myself, figuring my heroic gesture will have you swooning at my feet at a later date." He brushed a finger across her lips. "You know how many cold showers I'll have to take after tonight? There isn't enough water in Lake Michigan."

"You're an idiot," she muttered. But the hurt had faded from her eyes.

"You're right." He curled an arm around her shoulder and steered her toward her bedroom. "You know how long I've been secretly lusting after you? It's been months, Ferguson. Months. And suddenly I get a conscience. I must be out of my mind."

The bed stood in a puddle of moonlight, the covers twisted and hanging to the floor. He eased her onto the mattress. But instead of lying down, she looked up at him.

"I wouldn't use you like that, Mac," she said softly.

He crouched next to her. "Hey, I've always wanted to be a sex slave." He trailed one finger down the center of her chest and hooked it in the waistband of the boxers. "But we'll save that game for some other time, okay?"

A faint smile flickered over her mouth. "I'm not sure you'd make a very good sex slave. You don't take orders very well."

"I would from you, A.J." He swallowed, the lightness vanishing. "I would from you."

She watched him for a moment, then laid her hand on his cheek. "Thank you," she whispered. "I'm glad you're here."

"Me, too."

A smile curved her mouth, then she lay down on the bed and pulled up the blankets. In moments her eyes were closed.

He leaned against the wall, watching her until he saw the steady rise and fall of her chest, heard her slow even breathing and knew she was asleep. He could leave, stretch out on the couch for what was left of the night.

But he didn't move. Shifting against the hard wall, he stretched out his legs and closed his eyes. He'd stay with her until morning.

CHAPTER EIGHT

TWO MORE WOMEN to place.

A.J. had been on the phone all day, calling women's shelters in nearby communities, trying to find spots for the women left homeless after the fire at Harbor House.

She dropped the phone back into its cradle and rubbed her forehead. A vicious headache pounded at her temples, and her eyes were gritty from lack of sleep.

Mac had been gone when she emerged from her bedroom that morning. As she'd slipped out of bed in the soft dawn light, she'd heard her front door closing quietly.

He'd stayed all night.

Then he'd sent a squad car to follow her into work.

Unsettled, restless, she'd tried to push him out of her head since then, with little success. Even through the work and the worry, he lingered there.

She closed her eyes and pushed thoughts of him away again. She had to finish.

The next shelter on the list was in the far western suburbs. A long, slow drive from Riverton, especially during afternoon rush hour.

Her head throbbing, she reached for the phone again. She'd drive the women out to the boonies herself. There was no way she'd leave them without somewhere to stay. Without a refuge, they might go back to their partners.

As she punched in the numbers for the shelter in Naperville, someone cleared his throat out in the bull pen.

"Hello? Is anyone here?"

Replacing the phone, she walked into the room. An older man stood on the periphery, his uncomfortable gaze sweeping the near-empty room. His expensive suit and tie looked out of place, as if he'd been heading for a board meeting and taken a wrong turn.

One of the patrol officers on the other side of the room started to rise. He sank back into his seat when she appeared.

"Can I help you?" she asked.

The man turned polite, cool eyes on her. "I'm looking for Pierce McDougal. Could you notify him he has a visitor?"

Her heartbeat stuttered at Mac's name. Ignoring the reaction, she studied the man who'd assumed she was a secretary. "I have no idea where Mac went. But you're welcome to leave a message." She nodded her head toward his desk. "That's his desk. I can't promise when he'll get back to you, but I know he will."

The man's lips tightened. "He didn't inform you of his plans?"

"I'm not his secretary." She reined in her temper and forced her coolness to match his own. "We work together. I'm the department's victim's advocate. Is there something I can help you with?"

"No, thank you. My business with Pierce is personal."

Her curiosity was piqued in spite of herself. Mac wasn't shy when it came to his opinions about rich people. And this guy was definitely a snob. What could he possibly want with Mac that was personal?

"Let me get you a piece of paper, then, and you can leave him a note."

"Don't bother."

She was halfway to her desk when he spoke, and she turned to look at him again. "It's no bother."

His lips tightened. "Thank you, but my business is best handled in person. I'll try again later."

"I could probably find his cell-phone number for you."

Scorn frosted his eyes. "That won't be necessary."

"Suit yourself."

His nod was curt and dismissive.

She studied the man who held himself so stiffly. His white hair was combed into place, his shoes gleamed with polish and his suit was expertly tailored. He was definitely not the type Mac would choose as a friend.

As she started back to her office, the man said, "May I ask you a question?" When she turned, she found him assessing her just as she'd done to him.

"Be my guest. I'll answer if I can."

"Does Pierce enjoy what he's doing?"

Silence hung between them for a long beat, then he stepped back. "Forgive me. That was too personal."

"Yes, it was. Still, it's an easy question to answer. Mac loves what he's doing. And he's very good at it."

He studied her face for another moment, then gave a sharp nod. "Thank you."

As he moved to leave, Mac and Jake walked into the office. Mac stopped dead.

"What are you doing here?" he demanded of the man.

"Pierce."

A.J. noticed a strain in the older man's voice that hadn't been there a moment ago.

"I have information you might find useful. About Doak."

"Is that right? To what do I owe this sudden attack of good citizenship?"

Mac hummed with antagonism, his hands curling into fists. A.J. pushed away from the wall and stepped between the two men. She touched his arm, drew back before she could reach for his hand. "You'll have to pardon Detective McDougal. He hasn't been himself lately."

"On the contrary, he appears to be exactly himself."

Mac shouldered past A.J. "Stay out of this, Ferguson."

Instead of backing away, she moved closer. She touched his arm again, found his rock-hard muscles quivering with tension. She let her hand linger.

Mac ignored her. "What do you have on Doak?"

"I remembered he had an account at the Taylor Evans bank. An account he was somewhat secretive about. He wrote me a check from there several weeks ago and asked me to cash it immediately, not show it to anyone. Were you aware of the account?"

"No. I'll look into it right away. Thank you," Mac muttered. It sounded as if the words stuck in his throat.

After a tense moment, he asked, "Why are you giving me this? Why are you ratting out your partner?"

"I am not 'ratting out' Doak. I simply want this unfortunate misunderstanding cleared up, as quickly as possible." The older man straightened his tie, his hand not quite steady.

"Afraid it's going to hurt your bottom line?" Mac asked.

The older man stared at him for a long moment. "Your mother wants you to come to dinner. Tomorrow, at seven o'clock." He glanced at A.J. "You can bring your friend." Without another word, he walked away.

Mother? Dinner? Was this Mac's father? A.J. watched the man until he disappeared into the stairwell.

"Mac…?" she began.

He whirled to face her. "Don't start on me, Ferguson. Don't say a word."

As he stormed past, she gave Jake a puzzled look. Mac's partner shrugged.

"Let's go, Donovan," Mac said, slamming a desk drawer. The sound bounced off the walls. "Or are you taking the rest of the day off?"

"You know, your sunny disposition is one of the things I love the most about you, Mac," Jake drawled. But there was sympathy in his eyes. "It makes for such a pleasant work environment."

"Screw you."

Mac's eyes snapped to A.J. "Don't leave this building by yourself. I expect you to be here when we get back."

Bristling at his overbearing tone, she said, "Then you'll be disappointed. I'm trying to find places for the women from the shelter, and the closest one is in Naperville. I'll be on my way there by the time you're finished at the bank."

He grabbed her wrist, his fingers tightening around it like a handcuff. "I'm warning you, A.J. Don't step out of here without me."

"How are you going to stop me?"

He reached into her office and snatched her car keys from the outside pocket of her purse. "That's how."

She moved into the doorway, blocking his exit from her office. "Give those back to me."

He shoved them into the pocket of his jeans. "You want them? Come and get them."

His eyes smoldered with temper, fueling her own. He was spoiling for a fight and it wasn't about her keys. The rational part of her mind understood that. But anger swelled inside her. Slamming the door behind her, she started toward him.

"Give me those keys," she ordered in a low, deadly voice. "Right now. *Pierce*."

Something dark and ugly flashed in his eyes. He backed toward the door, watching her. "I don't think so. You're not going anywhere today."

The tight control she kept on her temper snapped and blood roared in her ears. She slapped her hands on her desk and her right hand closed around a small paperweight shaped like a globe. Without thinking, she picked it up and flung it at his head. He dodged to the side just in time.

The paperweight crashed into the wall with a sharp thud and fell to the floor.

A.J. stared at the smooth depression in the wallboard where the paperweight had hit. The rage drained out of her in a sudden, shocking rush, leaving her shaking.

She sank into her chair and pressed her fingers to the bridge of her nose. "Leave the keys and get out of here, Mac." She spoke in a whisper without looking at him.

Mac studied the point of impact. The wicked crack still rang in his ears. "What the hell was that about?" he asked.

"You made me lose my temper." Even muffled through her hands, he heard the stunned shock in her voice. "I never lose my temper." She raised her head and her eyes were huge and dark, the pupils dilated. "Leave."

His anger and frustration with the case, with his father, his humiliation because A.J. had witnessed their confrontation, all drained away. He walked over to her desk and squatted next to her. He wanted to touch her, to absorb some of the pain reflected in her face.

She wouldn't allow it. He could practically see her scrambling to rebuild the fences.

Not this time. "That's a hell of an arm you've got there, Ferguson. Where have you been hiding? The Cubs could use you."

When she lifted her head, he saw a spark of anger flare in her eyes. Then she caught herself. "You're not going to provoke me again. Go away, Mac."

"Not going to happen." He rocked back on his heels as he studied her. "You look like someone just died. What's the big deal? You lost your temper. You threw something at me. I deserved it. End of story."

She watched him steadily, her eyes unreadable. "Bad things happen when I lose my temper, Mac."

"Like what?"

She turned her head. "You don't want to know."

He nudged her chin until she looked at him again. "You think I can't handle your temper? That you're going to scare me off if you blow up at me? I'm tougher than that, A.J." His hand tightened on her chin, then smoothed down her throat. "I can handle a temper tantrum."

"Can you?"

"Count on it." His mouth curved up in a half smile. "I know about tempers. Even though I'm notorious for my easygoing ways and mild disposition."

Almost as if against her will, she smiled a tiny smile. "I've always admired that about you."

He watched her for an instant. She wouldn't quite meet his eyes.

"I'm sorry, A.J. I shouldn't have taken your keys." He placed them on her desk. "I shouldn't have snapped orders at you." He paused, let the moment stretch out. "Want to know why I did?"

Finally she met his gaze. "Yes," she whispered.

"I'm terrified. All I can think about is Doak with his hands on you. Hurting you."

"How am I supposed to stay angry at you when you say something like that?"

"You're not. You made a mistake. I did, too. Now we move on."

"Why are you so angry with your father?"

"This discussion isn't about my father." As the jolt of anger hit him, he admired her quickness in changing his focus and guessing his relationship with his visitor.

"I'm sorry." Her eyes held only pity now.

"Nothing to be sorry about."

"Yes, there is. Broken faith between parents and their children is always sad."

"I don't need that social-worker therapist crap."

"Maybe that's exactly what you need."

"The hell it is. I suppose your relationship with your parents is nothing but sweetness and light."

She looked down at her desk and twined her fingers together, her knuckles turning white. "My parents have nothing to do with this."

"I suppose you don't ever fight with them?"

She squeezed her fingers together, then carefully untangled her hands. Red spots on the backs of her hands marked the places where she'd been pressing. When she raised her head, her eyes were expressionless. "My parents are dead."

Horrified at his gaffe, he reached for her instinctively. "I'm sorry, A.J."

Slipping away from him, she took a deep, trembling breath. "It's all right. We weren't talking about me, anyway. We were talking about you."

"Look. I'm sorry I was rude. I'm sorry I tried to take your keys. Now can we drop it?"

"It's forgotten," she said too quickly. Her guarded eyes betrayed her easy words.

She turned away for a long moment, and when she faced him he saw nothing but mild inquiry in her eyes.

"Are you going to your parents' for dinner tomorrow?"

"I don't know," he muttered.

"Whatever went wrong between you and your father, he took the first step by coming here with information about Doak. It wouldn't kill you to go to dinner."

"Believe me, one dinner isn't going to fix what's wrong between us."

He couldn't believe he'd said that. He'd told no one about his relationship with his parents. Not even Jake.

"Probably not. But it's a start." Her mouth curved into a smile. "Give him a little credit. He's trying. He even invited one of your coworkers."

"Forget it," he said, his voice flat. "There's no way I'd subject you to that."

"Burdens shared are easier to carry."

"Not this burden."

In spite of his words, he wanted her with him tomorrow night. He wanted her there as a connection to his real life, as a reminder of what was important. He wanted her there as a shield between him and his parents, to keep the conversation civilized. But mostly he just wanted to be with her.

And because that was selfish and a little frightening, he stood and picked up the paperweight, determined to lighten the mood.

"You've got yourself quite a weapon here." He nodded at the dent in the wall. "You going to call maintenance to fix that?"

"No. I'll leave it there as a reminder."

"A reminder of what a jerk I am?"

"I don't need a reminder of that. I witness it daily." She softened her words with a tiny smile, then glanced at the wall. "It's a reminder about what happens when I lose control."

He studied her, pieces of the A.J. puzzle shifting once again. "You don't like losing control, do you?"

"Does anyone?"

"Some handle it better than others."

"You're right. I don't handle it well." She sighed and sat back in her chair. "What if you left with my keys and there was an emergency? What if I needed my car?"

"There are plenty of guys who'd love to help you."

"Believe me, I don't need that kind of help."

"You want the guys to back off? The next time one of them comes on to you, just throw that paperweight at his head. That'll cool them all off in a hurry."

Her gaze moved again to the wall behind him. "I haven't lost my temper in a long time."

"I like passion. Especially in you. But temper's not the kind of passion I had in mind."

"It's the only kind you're likely to get," she retorted.

"I guess I imagined last night, then."

She wrapped her arms around herself, her hand hovering over the wound on her side. "Last night was a mistake," she said in a low voice.

"You think so?"

"I know so."

"That sounds like a dare to me, Ferguson." He moved closer, watching her eyes darken, her pulse jump, her lips part.

"Don't tell me. You like dares." She tried to sound nonchalant, but her voice caught in her throat.

"Oh, yeah. Almost as much as I like passion. And challenges."

She swallowed, her throat rippling. Her breasts rose and fell beneath her jacket. Finally she looked away.

Her hand shook slightly as she picked up her keys. "I'm going home. I can call shelters from there. You can walk me to my car if you think it's necessary."

He allowed her to move around him, but he didn't take his eyes off her. "Oh, it's necessary," he said softly.

As she reached for the light switch, her fingers skimmed over the depression made by her paperweight. Then, straightening her shoulders, she walked out of the office and into the bull pen.

He followed her into the parking lot. She faltered at the edge of the asphalt and swept her gaze from side to side. He moved closer and dropped an arm over her shoulders, steering her toward her car.

"No bogeymen here tonight," he said.

She glanced over at him, shadows of old pain in her eyes. "There are always bogeymen."

He put his hands on her shoulders, drew her around to face him. "There don't have to be, A.J."

She gave him a sad smile. "I wish that was true."

Without looking at him again, she slid into her car and closed the door.

He put his hands on the open window. "I'll follow you home. You can tell me why you don't like to lose your temper."

"I don't want to talk about it. Don't crowd me, Mac."

"You're not going home by yourself," he answered.

"It's broad daylight. There will be lots of people around. And you and Jake have to check out the bank lead."

"The bank will be open for a while yet. I want to follow you home, A.J." He skimmed a finger along her arm, felt a response shiver through her. "For me."

"Suit yourself," she said, shrugging. But her hands trembled on the steering wheel.

He straightened as she put her car in gear, pulled away from him. "I intend to, A.J.," he murmured to himself. "And I'm beginning to think you suit me just fine."

CHAPTER NINE

TWENTY MINUTES LATER, as they walked down the hall to her apartment door, a call came over Mac's radio. After checking all the rooms in her apartment, he turned to her. "You're saved by the radio," he murmured, sliding his hands down her arms to her hands. He brushed his lips over hers, and leaned closer when she involuntarily opened her mouth. Another call came, and he tore himself away. "I'll be back, A.J.," he said, his eyes dark. "I'm not going to forget where we were."

But he didn't come back that night. A.J. prowled her apartment for too long, wondering where he was, irritated with herself for acting like a teenage girl. She told herself that she was relieved he'd decided to drop the subject. Still, disappointment that he hadn't returned kept her awake.

The next morning, she felt unsettled as she pulled into a parking spot at the station. Jittery from lack of sleep and too much caffeine, she closed her eyes and took a deep breath. Keeping her sunglasses on over her aching eyes, she opened the door and stepped out.

Before she could lock her car, a now-familiar black SUV drove into the lot and turned into the space next to hers. Mac jumped out, closing the door carefully behind him. Exhaustion had carved deep grooves on his face, and his eyes were red and strained.

"Running away from me again, Ferguson?" he said, leaning against the front of his truck and crossing his arms over his chest.

"Of course not," she said, trying to keep her voice light. Her fingers tightened on the handle of her briefcase. "I called your cell phone and left a message that I was heading into work, didn't I?"

"But you didn't wait for me. Why was that?" He pushed away from the truck and started toward her.

She licked her suddenly dry lips and took a gulp of her too-hot coffee. It burned all the way down her throat. "I figured you'd meet me here."

"A.J., A.J., A.J." He shook his head. "What am I supposed to think?"

"What do you mean?" she asked, uneasy with his light, teasing tone.

"You call me, then run away before I can follow you. Then you stop for coffee on the way in to work."

"What's wrong with that?" She glanced down guiltily at the cup in her hand.

"You didn't get any for me." He smiled at her and her heart jumped in her chest. "I guess I'll have to have some of yours."

He took the cup from her unresisting hand and placed his mouth exactly where hers had been. His eyes held hers as he took a drink.

She watched in helpless fascination at the ripple of muscles in his throat as he swallowed. He started to hand the cup back to her, then stopped.

He looked down at the cup, then back at her. Without taking his eyes off her, he licked a drop of coffee from the rim of the cup. "I can't get enough of that," he murmured.

"What are you doing, Mac?" she whispered.

"I'm talking to one of my colleagues," he answered, his eyes hooded. "What does it look like I'm doing?"

She was completely out of her depth. Beneath the edgy nerves, an unfamiliar excitement hummed through her.

"You're flirting with me."

"Flirting? With A.J. Ferguson?" He shook his head again. "Now that's crazy talk. Everyone in the department knows what happens when you flirt with A.J. Ferguson."

"What's that?"

"You take your life in your hands." He moved a step closer. "But then, I've always been a risk taker."

"I thought you were going to come by last night," she said, unable to look away from him.

His pupils dilated. "I'm glad you missed me."

"Did you get a call?" She struggled to steer the conversation back to impersonal topics.

He closed his eyes and sighed, reverting to the detective. "Yeah. We found the gas can Doak used to start the fire at the shelter."

"Oh, no." Her stomach was in knots. "Are you sure it was Doak?"

"His fingerprints were all over the can. He tossed it under the porch of a house close to the shelter. That's where I was most of the night."

She studied his face, saw the fatigue there and the dark shadow of beard on his cheeks. He hadn't shaved before coming to work.

And he hadn't changed his clothes since yesterday, either. The black T-shirt with the rugby-team logo was rumpled and creased, as if he'd slept in it.

He *had* slept in it, she realized with another spurt of guilt. The second night in a row he hadn't seen his bed.

"And when you were finished, you spent the rest of the night in your truck watching my apartment, didn't you?" she asked quietly.

"I didn't want him doing the same thing to your apartment building."

"I don't want you sleeping in your truck to protect me," she said.

"I don't have to sleep in the truck."

Desire shivered through her. She wanted to dive into his eyes, to plumb those blue depths and discover what Mac kept so carefully hidden.

She blinked and broke the spell. She'd never been a good swimmer.

"My couch is barely more comfortable than the truck," she said, trying to keep her voice light. "That's not an experience you want to repeat."

"I wasn't talking about the couch."

In addition to the stubble and wrinkled shirt, his hair hadn't seen a comb this morning, and there was a spot on his jeans. He shouldn't have looked sexy. But he did.

He made her feel wild and reckless, made her body sing with need.

And that scared her to death.

"I'm sorry," she whispered. "I'm not used to this." She swallowed. "To what seems to be happening here."

"Yeah, I noticed." He tilted his head. "Why is that, A.J.? I figured there'd be a swarm of guys hanging around, begging for your attention."

"Nope," she said. "No swarm."

"How come?" He ran a finger down her nose, pushed a curl of hair behind her ear.

"I don't get involved with men I work with. And even if I did, I don't do meek and mild."

"Now there's a news flash." He gave her his killer grin, the one that made her knees weaken. "Here's another one. Some guys don't want meek and mild."

"We all know what you want, McDougal," she said, trying to lighten the moment. "You and your arm candy are legends in the department."

"You have no idea what I want, Ferguson."

Her mouth went dry. "Are you going to tell me?"

"Do you want to know?"

"Yes," she whispered.

He moved a step closer, crowding her against the car. "I've developed a craving for tall, leggy brunettes with attitude." The heat in his eyes lit tiny fires under her skin. "And you know how it is with cravings."

"How is it?" She held her breath.

"You just have to satisfy them."

As his mouth brushed over hers, a car door slammed behind them. Mac straightened, his gaze locked on hers, his face taut. "This is the wrong place for this conversation. Some cravings can't be satisfied in public."

He picked up the briefcase she must have dropped and gave her a slow, seductive smile. "Remember where we left off, A.J."

He stepped away, and her legs wobbled as she walked beside him into the building. He was careful not to touch her, but it didn't matter. She was aware of nothing but him. His scent, his heat, his presence had combined to steal her common sense and her caution.

She could think of nothing but continuing their conversation.

LATER THAT MOR   . A.J. stepped out of her car at the house in Chicag   south of Riverton—that now sheltered Mindy Talbott. Mac pulled in behind her and got out of his truck. He'd insisted on accompanying her, and she hadn't argued.

"How long do you think you'll be?" he asked.

"I'll stay as long as Mindy wants to talk."

"You care about her, don't you?"

"Of course I do. That's my job."

"We all care about our jobs. You care deep down. Like what happens to these women is vitally important to you. Like you're invested in their lives."

"I *am* invested in their lives. There's nothing more important than getting these women away from their abusers," she answered quietly. "Nothing more important than preventing more violence."

He gave her a quick half smile. "There's that passion again. No wonder I can't resist you."

Her stomach flipped. Before she could answer, he stepped into his truck. "Call me when you're ready to leave."

Aware of Mac watching her, she walked to the house. The doorbell rang inside, and finally the door opened. "I'm A.J. Ferguson." She introduced herself to the woman standing there. "I called a while ago. I'm here to see Mindy Talbott."

"She's in the living room," the woman said.

As A.J. stepped into the house, she heard the roar of Mac's truck driving away. Mindy sat on a couch, reading a book. She looked up when A.J. walked into the room.

"Hello, Mindy. How are you doing?"

"Better." She touched her face, where the bruises were turning yellow and green.

"You look like you're feeling better." A.J. sat down next to her. "I'm glad you called. What can I do for you?"

"Give me back my son. I want Jamie here with me."

"I can't do that, Mindy. I'm sorry."

"He's so little," she whispered. "And so afraid. He needs me."

"Yes, he needs his mother, but he's safe where he is right now, and that's the most important thing," she said gently. "Cissy is taking care of him. I saw him the other day and he seems comfortable with her."

"Did he…did he mention me?"

"He misses you, Mindy. He wants to be with you."

The woman lowered her head and tears rolled down her cheeks. "I thought Jamie would never want to see me again," she admitted. "I failed him. I didn't protect him from Doak."

"Of course he wants to see you. He loves you."

Mindy circled A.J.'s wrist with surprisingly strong fingers. "Keep Doak away from him. Doak will hurt him. Maybe even kill him."

"Doak won't get anywhere near Jamie," A.J. promised.

"Doak has been acting strange around Jamie. That's what I wanted to tell you. He'd started to ask where Jamie was. He wanted to know all about him. He'd never been very interested in Jamie before." Her eyes held fear and desperation. "I liked it when Doak ignored

Jamie. Lately it seemed as if Doak hated Jamie. Hated his own son."

"Jamie is safe," A.J. said firmly. "No one knows where he is except me and Detective McDougal."

Mindy's fingers tightened painfully. "You make sure he stays safe."

Thank goodness Mindy was getting some spine back. "Have you remembered anything else that could help us catch Doak?" A.J. asked.

"No." She pressed her lips together. "I don't know where Doak would go or who he'd see. I never did."

"You won't be safe until we find him," A.J. reminded her.

"You don't think I'd help you if I could?" Mindy stared into A.J.'s eyes, anger stirring in her own. "You don't think I know I should have protected Jamie? Then you know nothing about being a mother."

As A.J. DROVE BACK to the station, she realized she was close to Jeanine Jamison's neighborhood. Impulsively, she decided to stop and see how the woman was doing.

The Jamisons lived in a tidy two-story house, painted white with black shutters on the windows. The landscaping was neat and well tended, and a huge maple tree shaded the front yard. The flower beds had been carefully weeded and mulched, and the bushes recently trimmed.

The doorbell echoed, but A.J. didn't hear footsteps coming to the door. She waited a moment, then rang it again. She was just about to leave when she heard someone fumbling with the lock on the door.

It opened a crack and she saw half of Jeanine's face, framed in the small space.

"Hi, Jeanine," A.J. said. "I was driving through your neighborhood and thought I'd see how things were going between you and Todd."

"We're fine, Ms. Ferguson. Thanks for coming by."

She started to close the door, sending alarm signals buzzing in A.J.'s ears. A.J. put out her hand and stopped the door. "What's wrong, Jeanine?"

The woman turned her face away. "Nothing."

Sick at heart, recognizing the behavior, A.J. gently pushed the door open. When Jeanine turned away, A.J. reached out and turned her around. A bruise darkened the woman's jaw, the discoloration continuing down her neck.

"What happened, Jeanine?" She struggled to hide her anger and the sickness gathering in her stomach.

"Nothing. I walked into a door," the woman answered too quickly. "It was dark and I didn't see it."

A.J. touched the bruise. "Todd hit you, didn't he?"

Jeanine's lips trembled. "He didn't mean to hurt me. It was an accident. I took his car keys away from him, and he got so angry that he started…he started throwing things." Her fingertips touched her jaw. "A book hit me."

"A book didn't hit you, Jeanine. Todd hit you with a book." She led the older woman toward a couch. Sitting down, she grasped Jeanine's hands. "I need to ask you something. Does your husband hit you?"

"No," she said instantly. "Hugh is wonderful. He even puts up with Todd."

A.J. narrowed her eyes, her interest sharpened. "Isn't he Todd's father?"

"Hugh is Todd's stepfather." Jeanine slid her eyes away. "I divorced Todd's father several years ago."

Pieces of the Jamison puzzle were falling into place. "Todd's father beat you, didn't he?" she asked, familiar sadness mixed with white-hot rage.

"Yes." Jeanine bent her head and tears gathered in her eyes. "I had to divorce him. He was poisoning Todd."

"And now Todd is doing the same things."

"He's just angry. He doesn't like Hugh. He wants me to get back together with his father."

"I wish you had told me. It would have been easier to understand what Todd was doing. Have you contacted that therapist yet?" A.J. asked.

"No. Todd said he wouldn't go see any…" Her face turned pink. "He doesn't want to see a therapist."

"All right." A.J. let her go. "Then here's the deal," she said briskly. "Todd now has two choices. He can come and see me, or the police will arrest him for domestic battery. If I don't like what he has to say, or if he refuses to cooperate with me, he'll still be arrested."

"He won't want to talk to you."

"That's his choice. But if I don't see Todd in my office by tomorrow, there will be a police officer at your door. Or at his school." She touched Jeanine's arm. "You tell him that. He wouldn't want to be arrested at school, in front of his friends."

"You can't do that." Jeanine stared at her, appalled. "He's still a child."

"He's an abuser, Jeanine." She hardened her heart against his mother's tears. "We have to stop him."

"You have no proof that he hit me! I'll say I walked into a door and no one can prove otherwise."

"I know that." A.J. closed her eyes, praying for the patience to cut through the excuses, the denials, the justifications. "I can have Todd arrested on suspicion of domestic battery. We won't be able to hold him unless you tell the truth. But we can scare him. We can make him get the help he needs." She softened her voice. "Todd needs help, Jeanine. You know it, too. That's why you came to me after he was arrested for fighting. I want to help him get it."

Jeanine Jamison's eyes were focused on nothing. When she looked back at A.J., there was a flicker of hope mixed with the pain and despair on her face.

"I'll try," she said in a low voice. "I'll try to make him come to see you."

"Tomorrow," A.J. said, her voice firm. "After that, all bets are off."

Todd was so young, barely more than a child himself, and he was already an abuser.

Maybe she could make a difference for this family, A.J. thought with a wisp of hope. Too often, all she could do was try to put the pieces back together and help rebuild shattered lives.

Maybe this time she could help a family heal itself before the ugliness swallowed them completely.

"All right," Jeanine said. "I'll do the best I can."

A.J. stood up to leave, taking one last look at Jeanine as she stepped out the door. Sadness and pity pressed down on her as the door closed behind her. Sadness for a broken family, sadness for another child betrayed and damaged by his father. And pity for the woman who had to make such difficult choices, choices no parent should have to face.

MAC LOOKED UP FROM HIS DESK as he heard A.J. walk up the stairwell. He knew it was A.J. even before she came through the door. Irritated with himself, with the awareness that hummed incessantly through everything he did, he threw down the file he'd been reading.

Her mouth drooped and her eyes were dark with sorrow. "A.J.," he said, getting to his feet before he realized it. "You okay?"

"I'm fine, Mac."

She answered without looking at him and continued walking into her office. He followed her.

"The hell you are. What happened?"

"Other than the fact that I just dealt with two victims

of domestic violence? That I talked to two women with bruised faces? Other than the fact that two children have been brutalized by their own fathers and their lives will never be the same?"

She tossed her briefcase onto the desk and threw herself into her chair. "Other than that, I'm peachy."

"No, you're not." He sat on the corner of her desk.

"I'm fine," she said again on a sigh. She gave him a weak smile. "Just hot and cranky."

"Tell me, A.J."

She closed her eyes. He was damn sure she was seeing Mindy Talbott's face in her mind.

"Mindy is worried about Jamie," she began. "Doak had been paying a lot of attention to him lately." She opened her eyes and they burned with anger. "Apparently that was unusual. She told me to keep him away from Doak. She's afraid Doak is going to hurt him. Or worse."

"What else?" he prompted.

"I stopped to see Jeanine Jamison on the way home. And don't say a word." She shot him a fierce look. "No one followed me there. Doak was nowhere around."

"And?" He'd deal with her detour later.

"And she had a bruise on the side of her face. Todd threw a book at her."

"Want me to send someone to pick him up?"

She shook her head. "I gave her until tomorrow to get him in to talk to me. If that doesn't work, then yeah.

You can pick him up. Preferably at school, where his friends can watch. And make sure they know he was hitting a woman."

"Good call. Nothing like a little humiliation in front of his friends to adjust the attitude of a teenager." He paused, studying her. "It's also a tough call. What happened to Ms. Bleeding Heart Softy Ferguson?"

"Todd is already an abuser," she said, her voice flat. "If he isn't stopped now, he's going to get worse. In a few years you'll be going on domestics to his house and taking his wife and kids to a shelter."

She reached for her briefcase and began stuffing files into it. "I'm going to go home, have a glass of wine and try to forget about today. If you want to follow me I'm too tired to argue with you."

"We've got a little problem with that," he began.

"What do you mean?"

"I can't keep an eye on you tonight."

"Don't worry about it. I'm not going anywhere."

"I have a better idea." He took a deep breath, realizing he'd planned to ask her all along. "Why don't you come with me instead?"

She gave him a puzzled look. "What do you mean?"

"Come with me to my parents' house for dinner. You were invited, after all," he said lightly.

She dropped a handful of files on the desk and stared at him. "You want me to come to dinner with you? At your parents' house?"

"Forget it." He backpedaled at the shocked look on her face. "Just kidding."

She continued to stare at him. "I don't think you were."

"I thought it would be like killing two birds with one stone."

"What do you mean?"

"I could keep an eye on you. And you could prevent more domestic violence."

She cocked her head and waited for him to continue.

"You can keep me and my father from killing each other."

She watched him for a moment, and he hated the pity in her eyes. He was just about to tell her to forget it when she sighed.

"Your father invited me because he thought we were involved. He made that clear. I don't want to give your parents the wrong idea."

"I don't care what kind of idea we give them." He inhaled deeply and took the plunge. "I'd like you to come with me."

"Why?"

Because he wanted her with him. Wanted her strength and her support. And was shaken at the realization. "Because two sets of eyes and ears are better than one," he pointed out, shrugging. "You can help me figure out if he's telling the truth about Doak. They're business partners. And they belong to the same country club."

She studied him for a long moment, and he had the uncomfortable feeling that she could see right into him, to his core and all the ugly history he didn't want to face alone.

"All right," she said, surprising him. "I'll go with you."

"Great," he said, trying to hide the pleasure that flooded him. "I'll pick you up at seven." He gave her a strained smile. "Wear your full body armor."

CHAPTER TEN

A.J. STUDIED THE HOUSE as Mac pulled his truck into the circular driveway. It was imposing. And cold. The shades were carefully half-drawn in all the white-shuttered windows, and the red brick seemed to reflect the setting sun rather than absorb it. Precisely trimmed bushes stood like short, squat sentinels across the front of the house.

"Here we are," Mac said. "Home sweet home."

"It's big," she said lamely, trying to find something positive to say about the house. "And well cared for. Your parents must spend a lot of time on maintenance."

He snorted. "Not their own time. McDougals don't do manual labor. They pay other people to do it for them."

Mac hesitated for a second after he climbed out. A.J. looked around while she waited. The tall oak trees surrounding the house should have softened it. Instead, they covered it with shadows.

Mac stared at the front door, then straightened his shoulders. "You ready for this?"

"Of course." He seemed utterly alone, standing on the steps to his parents' home, and she wanted to reach out to him. He moved away before she could.

The door chimes had barely stopped ringing when the door opened. The woman who stood there gave them a nervous smile. "Pierce. Come in." She stood to one side. "This must be your friend."

"This is A.J. Ferguson. A.J., this is my mother, Edith."

A.J. held out her hand. "It's a pleasure to meet you, Mrs. McDougal."

The older woman wore black linen slacks and a pale blue silk blouse that reeked of money. The pearls at her throat and on her ears gleamed in the light, lustrous and perfect. Her short, frosted hair was meticulously styled. It wouldn't dare subject Edith McDougal to a bad hair day.

As Mac's mother shook hands, she ran an assessing eye over A.J. and gave her a smile with no real warmth behind it. "Come in, dear."

Suddenly self-conscious, A.J. brushed at the lightweight, flowery skirt she wore and smoothed a hand over her curls. Maybe it hadn't been such a good idea to come here with Mac.

Mac's father walked up behind his wife. Edith inclined her head. "You've already met my husband Pierce, I believe."

"Yes," A.J. murmured. She leaned past Mac's mother to shake his father's hand and caught a whiff of the woman's expensive perfume.

Mac stood to the side with his hands jammed casually in his pockets, but his face was tight and tense. Without thinking, she moved to stand next to him. "Thank you for inviting me," she murmured.

Edith gave them a speculative look then closed the door. "Come into the living room."

A couch and chairs sat at precise angles, separated by wooden tables with surfaces polished to a high sheen. Carefully selected objets d'art were placed on the tables and the fireplace mantel. There were no family mementos or pictures in the room. As they sat on hard couches, Edith turned to A.J. with a stiff smile. "You young people are so fond of nicknames. What's your given name, dear?"

A.J. felt her expression harden. "My name is A.J."

"Doesn't it stand for something?"

"No." She pressed her lips together.

Edith tilted her head. "A.J. is an odd name to give a girl."

"I never thought of myself as odd."

With a tiny nod that acknowledged A.J.'s victory but promised a rematch, Edith turned to Mac. "What have you been up to, Pierce?"

After a few minutes of polite, forced conversation, a young woman in a black uniform came to the door and nodded to Mac's mother. Edith stood up. "Dinner is ready."

The meal was uncomfortable, punctuated by talk in

awkward starts and stops. Mac's father carved a piece
of rare beef and handed plates around the table. A.J.'s
stomach rebelled as she stared at the bloody meat on
her plate. Pushing it around with her fork, she concen-
trated on the delicate scalloped potatoes and the thin
green beans. As forks clinked against china, she searched
desperately for a neutral topic of conversation.

Mac, watching her, must have noticed her discom-
fort, because he asked, "What have you been up to,
Mom?"

Edith gave him a grateful smile and began to talk
about her garden club's latest fund-raiser. The three
McDougals ate their rare beef and pretended to be a
family. When the voices eventually faltered to an awkward stop, A.J. turned to Mac's father. "What exactly
do you do, Mr. McDougal?"

"I'm in finance. I arrange monetary backing for large
projects."

"In the old days he would have been called a robber
baron," Mac said, but there was no heat in his voice.

"I hardly qualify for that club," his father answered
with a forced smile. "I'm afraid I'm not in the same
league as Rockefeller and Carnegie."

That subject exhausted, silence threatened again, but
Edith turned to A.J. "And what do you do, dear?"

"I work with Mac at the police department," she answered. "I'm the victim's advocate."

Out of the corner of her eye she saw Mac's father

tense at the word *police*. Edith tilted her head politely. "How interesting. What does a 'victim's advocate' do?"

"I help people who have been victims of a crime. Sometimes, all they need is someone to talk to. If they need more than my training as a social worker can provide, I refer them to the agencies and organizations that can help them. Occasionally I sit in when a crime victim is questioned by the police or accompany them to court during a trial." She shrugged. "I guess you could say I'm the jack-of-all-trades at the department."

"Your work sounds fascinating."

"It is."

"A.J.'s most recent customers were Mindy and Jamie Talbott," Mac said.

The sound of a fork clattering to a plate reverberated in the sudden silence. Both of Mac's parents tensed and the temperature around the dining-room table plunged.

Mac's father deliberately picked up his fork. "How is your investigation going, Pierce?" he asked.

"It's going great. I expect to have Doak locked up real soon."

"I'm glad your job is going well," his father answered stiffly.

"Doak behind bars will make it better."

"You don't need to act so delighted about it."

"Why not? That's my job—putting criminals in jail."

"I know what your job is. There's no need to taunt

me with it," Mac's father said, his eyes glittering with sudden fury "That's why you came to the club, isn't it? You could have talked to me privately. But you wanted to rub my nose in it. You wanted all my friends to see my son, the policeman. You wanted to humiliate me. Just like you always have."

"I'm sorry my job humiliates you." A muscle twitched in Mac's jaw. "You'd sing a different tune if you needed the police. But I don't care. You know why? Your job humiliates me. So I guess we're even."

"Pierce, your father shouldn't get excited like this," Edith said.

For the first time tonight, A.J. saw cracks in the woman's perfect facade. Her lips were pale where she'd chewed off her lipstick, and her eyes, drenched with pain, moved from her husband to her son. When Mac began to stand, Edith laid a hand on his arm.

"Don't go. Please. We have an Alleghretti cake for dessert."

She turned to A.J. with a tight smile. Eyes that were identical to Mac's silently pleaded with her. "That was always his favorite."

"Really?" A.J. said, her voice desperately bright. "What kind of cake is it?"

While Edith babbled about white cake, buttercream frosting and a chocolate-ganache topping, A.J. watched Mac. Fury still churned in his eyes. When he caught her gaze, he slapped his hands on the table and began to stand.

"A.J. and I have to leave," he said.

"Can we wait until after dessert?" A.J. asked still in that brittle, too-bright voice. "I'd like to taste a piece of your favorite cake."

Recognition of her ploy was in his eyes, and he stared at her for a long moment. Then he looked at his mother and nodded as he sank back into his chair. "Alleghretti cake sounds good."

Edith gave A.J. a grateful smile. "Let me clear these plates and I'll get the cake."

A.J. rose to help her, but Edith shook her head sharply. "Please sit down. I'll be right back."

Mac's mother returned carrying a cake. The sheet cake in the clear glass pan was far from the elegant dessert A.J. had expected. It looked homey and down-to-earth. The kind of cake any mother would make for her son.

Had Edith McDougal actually baked the cake for Mac instead of having the cook do it for her?

Even if she had, the tableau—elegant woman holding cake—only emphasized the differences in the homes A.J. and Mac had grown up in. Her family had never had cake. They couldn't afford it, let alone someone to bake it for them.

But then again, there'd never been anything to celebrate in her childhood.

Mac stared at the slice of cake on his plate. Then he looked up at his father. "Let's cut to the chase," he said. "Why did you ask me to come to dinner tonight?"

"Your mother wanted you to come. Do I need more reason than that?"

"You never do anything without a reason. You wanted to find out about the investigation, didn't you?"

"I do business with Doak," his father said, his voice tight. "What happens to him affects me."

"And you're using me to get the dirt."

"Information is important in my business."

"It's important in my business, too. And you haven't been very forthcoming with any about Doak."

"The man is my business partner. I know nothing about his personal life."

"You want to know about the case? Here's something you can take to the bank. Doak is going to prison, and none of his rich, influential friends can do a thing about it. Is that what you wanted to hear?"

"I assumed you'd have some loyalty to your parents." Mac's father wiped his mouth with a heavy linen napkin. "I see I was wrong."

"Loyalty? You mean the kind you have for me?" Mac slapped his hand on the table. The glass of wine in front of him toppled over, the ruby-red liquid cascading over his cake and onto the tablecloth.

He stared at the mess for a moment, then looked at his mother. "I'm sorry, Mom," he said, his voice tight, then he pushed away from the table. "A.J. and I need to go. We both have work to do tonight."

Profound sadness crossed his mother's face and was

quickly hidden. "I'm glad you could both join us to-night," she said. "I enjoyed meeting you, A.J."

"Thank you for inviting me," A.J. replied. She folded her napkin carefully and set it on the table. "The meal was delicious."

"Pierce, would you like a piece of cake to take home?" Edith asked.

A.J. could see the curt refusal in Mac's eyes. But he took a deep breath. "That would be great, Mom."

Edith wrapped the cake in one of the napkins, then handed it to Mac. He shifted it from hand to hand as he waited for everyone to rise from the table.

Edith moved next to her son as they walked toward the front door. She said something to Mac in a low voice and Mac nodded stiffly.

A.J. walked with Mac's father. On an impulse, she turned to him and said, "You should be very proud of Mac. He's an honorable man and a credit to his family."

The older man looked at her with unreadable eyes. "He would have been more of a credit to his family if he'd gone into law or joined my business, as I'd wished."

"But he wouldn't have done as much good as he's doing now," she murmured. "And he wouldn't have been as happy."

"How can you know that?"

"Mac loves what he does," she said. "And he does it well. Isn't that all a parent can hope for his child?"

"A child's actions reflect on his parents. In our circles, a man with Pierce's abilities and advantages is expected to make something of himself."

"Then I'm sure you're proud and thankful that Mac has."

Pierce McDougal didn't answer, but he gave her a speculative look.

Mac's mother stood in the door, facing her son. She reached out to him tentatively, and he bent down and kissed her cheek. A.J. turned to shake his father's hand.

"You care about my son." His eyes were measuring. "But you didn't tell us anything about your background."

"I'm a colleague of Mac's," she said easily. "We all care about one another."

Pierce's cool gray eyes swept over her once, then he nodded. "Thank you for coming tonight."

She murmured her thanks to both of Mac's parents, then hurried down the steps to Mac's car, where he stood holding the door open for her. He closed it, then quickly got in, started the car and drove away. He didn't look back.

A muscle ticked in his jaw and he stared out the windshield, his hands fiercely gripping the steering wheel. Finally, stopped at a traffic light, his shoulders sagged and he let out a hard breath.

"I had no right to subject you to that, A.J."

"It's all right," she said, trying to banish the sympa-

thy she felt for him. Mac would be angry and humiliated if he saw it. "If I was able to prevent any blood-
shed, I'm glad I joined you."

He didn't say anything as he drove through the quiet
streets. When they pulled into the parking lot of her
apartment, he switched off the truck, then faced her.

"Thank you for the things you said to my father."

"They're all true," she answered. "You might be
stubborn and annoying, but you're a damn good detective. Your father needs to hear that."

"He doesn't want to hear it, but I appreciate the effort."

She couldn't read his expression in the shadowy
light. "Why doesn't he want to hear it?" she asked.
"Why isn't he proud of what you do?"

"It's a long story."

"I've always liked a good story," she said, giving him
a slight smile.

He turned to look out the window, his profile set in
hard lines. "This isn't a good one."

"Why don't you let me decide that?" She slid out of
the truck and went over to his side. "Come on upstairs
and have some coffee."

He simply stared at her for a moment, and she braced
herself for a quick, curt refusal. Then, to her surprise,
he jumped out of the truck and slammed the door.

"I know you, Ferguson. You're like a dog with a bone.
If I don't spill my guts, you'll chew at me until I do."

"Now there's a pleasant image."

He didn't say anything more until they'd walked into her apartment. Turning on the lights, she headed for the kitchen. "Is coffee all right?"

"I'd rather have that wine you mentioned this afternoon."

"Coming right up."

A minute later she handed him a glass of wine, then settled herself on the couch with her own. After a moment's hesitation, he sat down at the other end.

"I shouldn't have taken you there," he said quietly.

"You didn't know what would happen."

"I knew damn well what would happen. I should have known they'd try to figure out who you were, if you were important."

She smiled. "Believe me, that didn't bother me."

"It should." He took a gulp of wine. "Although my mother did ask one question I'm curious about myself. "What *does* A.J. stand for?"

The edge of a fearful memory prodded her. "It's my legal name."

"Legal. Really?" He raised an eyebrow, suddenly all cop.

"It's not important."

He nodded slowly. "All right. I can wait until you're ready."

"We weren't talking about me anyway," she said, her voice too high. She didn't want to think about her name. "Do visits to your parents always end up in a fight?"

"Usually worse than that. My father toned it down because we weren't alone."

"How can they be so blind, so unwilling to accept you?"

"I've always known what's important to them—their place in the community, their image. I tarnished that image when I refused to go to law school after I finished college. When I joined the police department, they thought it was the end of the world. Their only child, Pierce McDougal the third, a cop. My father could barely hold his head up in the country club."

"That's ridiculous. No one is that narrow-minded and rigid anymore."

"You saw him tonight. Intolerant bigotry is alive and well in Riverton." He swirled the wine in his glass. "The hell of it is, I'm as bad as my father. He's right. I did go to the country club to rub his nose in it. I could have talked to him privately."

"You had other reasons for going to the country club. You're looking into the disappearance of that waitress. It only makes sense that you would need information."

"Are you defending me, A.J.?"

"I don't think you need to be defended."

"No? You defended me to my father. Next you'll be saying that my parents were thrilled to see me tonight."

"Your mother was glad you were there."

"She wants to tell her club friends that her son came over for dinner. They keep track of stuff like that. Having her son come for dinner and bringing a woman will earn her points."

"That's not true. She baked your favorite dessert."

"She had the cook bake it."

"That was a homemade cake, Mac. No professional cook would send that out of the kitchen. Your mother baked that cake herself."

"I'll call her tomorrow and thank her," he said gruffly. "But it doesn't change a thing.

"A.J., don't try to defend either of them. I don't come from a loving, stable home and nothing you can say will change that. When I was growing up, my only value was as a weapon. They used me to stab at each other. And when I became an adult, they wanted to use me in their prestige contests with their friends. I should have known better than to go there for dinner. I shouldn't have taken you."

"I'm glad you did."

"Why is that? So you can make me the subject of a case study? Get a paper out of me?"

"Of course not."

"Then why would you be glad to sit through that?"

"I'm glad I was there for you. I'm glad you didn't have to endure that on your own."

Something new entered his eyes, pushing away the anger. "Yeah, well, thanks."

"He's going to regret it, you know," she said softly.

"I doubt it."

"At the very least, you've learned how not to raise your own kids."

"Kids? Yeah, I've learned that lesson real well. No way am I bringing a kid into this world."

"That's very sad," she said.

"No, it's smart."

She said nothing, and he finished his wine in a gulp, then set the glass on a table. "I'll let you get some sleep. Sorry I kept you up while I spilled my guts. I feel like a damn fool."

"You shouldn't. I'm glad you told me."

"Just another one of your customers, right, Ferguson?"

"No, a friend. You were there the other night when I needed someone. Now it's my turn to listen to you. That's what friends are for."

He kept his gaze on hers and leaned closer. The air seemed full of tiny bursts of lightning. And she couldn't remember how to breathe.

"You're more than a friend, A.J., and I think you know it."

"We work together, Mac," she whispered. Her fingers trembled as they pleated her skirt. "And there are a million other reasons why it's not a good idea."

"You think I haven't counted those reasons, too?" he asked. "You and me? That would border on criminally dumb." His mouth curved. "We'd spend half our time fighting."

"You're right."

"But the other half of the time… You know what we'd do the other half of the time."

"Yes," she whispered. She'd never wanted a man like this, never needed a man like this. A deep hunger filled her.

"I managed to keep my hands off you the other night. Touching you now would be asking for trouble." He was so close she could feel the heat from his body.

His gaze slid from her eyes to her mouth. "Good thing I like trouble."

He covered her mouth with his.

CHAPTER ELEVEN

HE TOOK THE WINEGLASS out of her hand and set it on the table behind her. Then he pulled her against him.

She wound her arms around his neck as he kissed her again. She couldn't think, couldn't remember all the reasons this was a mistake. All she knew was the taste of him, the feel of him.

One of them dragged in a ragged breath. She couldn't tell who. Before she could figure it out, he was kissing her again. He tasted like the wine they'd shared, rich and sharp.

He eased her down on the couch, and her muscles trembled with anticipation. He settled on top of her, his welcome weight pressing her into the cushions. She remembered the sight of him, sleeping on this couch, remembered his broad shoulders and tousled hair. She burrowed a hand beneath his shirt. She needed to touch him, to feel that warm skin and hard muscle against her palm.

"What's your name, A.J.?" he whispered. "Your real name. I want to say it while I touch you."

"It's A.J.," she said. "Just A.J."

With a groan he shifted his weight from her, eased to one side and ran his hand down her body, over her breasts. He tested their weight, teased one finger over her nipple. Even through her blouse and bra, the sensation was almost unbearable. She arched into his hand, whimpering against his mouth.

"I could get addicted to touching you, just A.J."

His fingers were shaking as he tried to shove the buttons through their holes. Finally he pushed her blouse apart and cool air caressed her chest. His mouth was desperate on hers as he fumbled with the clasp of her bra.

When it fell open and her breasts tumbled into his hands, he sucked in his breath and lifted his head.

"So beautiful," he whispered. "You're so beautiful, A.J."

He held her gaze while his hand covered one breast, his palm circling slowly over the nipple. With a shock, she realized that the ragged little cries echoing in her ears were coming from her. He bent his head to her breast, and the feel of his mouth on her had her aching for more. Restlessly he trailed his hand down her belly, down her thigh. She wrapped her leg around his, pulling him against her.

He bunched the fabric of her skirt and tugged at it, but then he froze. "A.J." He lifted his head, his breathing shallow. "A.J. Wait. Stop. Your beeper."

She wanted to scream with frustration. She closed her eyes and shuddered as she became aware of the insistent tones of her beeper.

Mac touched her face with an unsteady hand. "Are you on call?"

She nodded without opening her eyes.

He lifted his weight off her. She wanted to drag him back down to her, into her.

She heard him rummaging in her purse, then he handed her the beeper and her cell phone.

She sat up, staring down at the number displayed on the beeper. Clicking it off, she threw it back into her purse.

"I'm sorry, Mac." She couldn't look at him. "So sorry. I didn't remember... I wasn't planning..."

"Shhh," he said, touching her lips with one finger. "No apologies. Make the call."

That was one advantage of having monkey sex on the couch with a coworker, she thought wildly. At least he understood about being on call.

Except they hadn't quite gotten to the monkey sex part.

She wasn't sure which upset her more—that she'd almost had sex with Mac. Or that she hadn't.

Her hands shook as she punched in the numbers on her cell phone. She looked down. Her blouse hung open, and her bra dangled from her arms.

She held the edges of her blouse together as she waited for the call to go through.

The phone stopped ringing and one of the Riverton detectives answered it. "We need you, A.J.," the woman began. While A.J. tried to listen, Mac fastened one button on her blouse, then another.

She swallowed heavily as he finished buttoning. Finally she closed the phone and dropped it back into her purse.

"I have to go. A domestic. The woman needs help." She took a steadying breath. "I'm sorry, Mac."

"Me, too."

"Maybe it's a good thing the call came through when it did," she said, looking down at her blouse. It was buttoned, crookedly, and he hadn't closed her bra. The sheer fabric did nothing to hide her hard nipples. "If Detective Jones had waited another couple of minutes, we would have been…"

He turned her face toward him. "I would have been inside you."

"I didn't invite you up here so I could seduce you," she said, holding his gaze with an effort.

"I'm crushed." He gave her a slow, sexy smile that deepened the dimple in his cheek. "And here I thought you'd been planning all night to get me into bed."

"I'm having a hard time figuring this out," she whispered. "Figuring myself out. A week ago I didn't even like you."

"It's been quite a week." His hand slipped to her cheek, cupped it. His eyes were steady on hers, reassuring. "We don't have to figure it out tonight," he said. "The great mysteries of the world take time."

"I don't do casual sex, Mac. Ever. This—" she gestured to the couch "—the other night, when I asked…" Her face flamed. "That's not me."

"You never lose control?"

"No! Not about something this important."

"You felt pretty out of control to me," he murmured.

She'd been helpless in his hands, unable to think, unable to reason, unable to do anything but feel and need.

Mac was right. She'd been completely out of control.

It terrified her.

"I need you to back off. I have to think," she said.

"Don't think too much, A.J. We're both adults. We're both unattached. I want you. You want me. What's so complicated?"

"You know perfectly well it's more complicated than that. We work together, for God's sake. What happens when it's over? How do we face each other every day?"

"Hell if I know. But it will be fun while it lasts."

"I'm not interested in fun while it lasts," she said quietly. "That's one of the reasons I've never gotten involved with anyone at work."

"Only one? What are the other reasons?"

She tensed. Mac was dangerous. She'd almost blurted out more than she intended. "There are too many to count," she said, standing. "And I have to get going."

He stood as well. "I'll take you."

"You don't have to do that." She didn't want the other detectives to see her arriving with Mac at this hour of the night. They would immediately jump to conclusions.

"Don't worry. They know I've been sticking close because of Talbott," he said, apparently reading her mind. "No one will think twice."

"I'm fine," she said firmly. "You can follow me to the scene, but there's no reason for you to stay." She let her gaze skim over his tired face, then looked away. "You need to sleep. I'll make sure one of the patrol officers follows me home."

"And you call me stubborn," he said lightly. "All right. Let's go."

"I need to change my clothes first."

His gaze lowered to her chest. "Yeah. You do. I'll wait."

She hurried into her bedroom, feeling his eyes on her until she closed the door. Hurriedly she threw on jeans, re-hooked her bra and covered it with a loose, dark T-shirt. In moments she was back in the living room, scooping up her purse and keys. She avoided looking at Mac.

"I'm ready."

Before she could escape from the apartment, Mac put his hands on the door, trapping her. She stood there, her hand on the doorknob, refusing to turn around.

His lips brushed over the nape of her neck and she shivered. "I didn't think you were a coward, A.J."

Slowly she faced him. "They're waiting for me."

"This won't take long."

He took her mouth again, pressing her against the door. She wanted to resist, to reestablish a barrier between them, but her knees weakened. After a moment, he stepped back. Her eyes fluttered open.

"Keep that in mind when you're doing your thinking," he said.

They didn't speak as they walked to her car. His headlights burned steadily in her rearview mirror as he followed her to the address she'd been given. When she pulled to the curb, he drove past, raising one hand.

She waited until he was out of sight, then she locked the car door behind her and walked into the brightly lit house.

THE NEXT AFTERNOON, Mac slouched in the passenger seat of Jake's car as they drove toward the station. "I'm sure glad we wasted half a day," he said sourly. They'd gotten the name of an old boyfriend of Helena Tripp. The waitress who'd given them the name had said Helena had had a rocky relationship with the young man.

The kid had claimed he hadn't seen or heard from Helena in a couple of months. They'd check his alibi, but it was rock solid. And since he and Jake had rousted the kid and a young woman out of bed, Mac was bet-ting that the kid had nothing to do with Helena's disappearance.

"Another one to mark off the list. We knew going in he was a long shot," Jake reminded him. "According to your waitress, it's been a while since Helena went out with the guy."

"She's not my waitress."

"My, my. We're grouchy today, aren't we? Did A.J. shut you down?"

"What's going on between me and A.J. is none of your damn business!"

Mac saw Jake's eyebrows rise. "So there *is* something going on between you and our lovely victim's advocate."

"Go to hell, Donovan."

He could feel Jake's gaze on him, but he refused to acknowledge it. The car pulled up to a stoplight and Jake shifted in the seat.

"You better not hurt her," he said softly. "Because if you do, I'll have to kick your ass."

Mac scowled at him, but Jake kept staring. Finally Mac sighed and looked away. "A.J. won't give anyone the chance to hurt her," he said. "Especially me."

"She's a wise woman."

"You think I want to get involved with her?" he snarled. "Damn complicated woman. I like it simple and clean. No muss, no fuss."

"If you're looking for simple, don't look at A.J."

"Yeah, well, maybe I don't have a choice," he muttered.

"That bad, huh?"

The car jerked away from the stoplight and Mac didn't answer. After a few minutes, he said, "I liked our relationship just fine. We yelled at each other once in a while and otherwise kept our distance." He scowled. "Since Talbott attacked her, everything's changed."

"Cheer up, son. Knowing you, I guarantee A.J. will be yelling at you again real soon."

"It's my fondest hope," he grumbled.

He hadn't been able to get her out of his head since he'd left her. As soon as he closed his eyes, he could taste her skin, her mouth. He could hear the tiny cries she made in the back of her throat when he touched her. And he could feel the way she rose up to meet his mouth, to fill his hands.

Just as vivid was his memory of the determination in her eyes when she moved away from him. When she told him sorry, she'd lost control, but it wouldn't happen again.

"Speaking of the devil," Jake said. "Where do you think she's going now?"

He nodded to the oncoming traffic. Mac caught a glimpse of A.J., speeding along in the opposite direction, and he let out a low, vicious curse.

"She's supposed to wait for me."

"Looks like she didn't." Jake's voice was cheerful.

"Turn around," Mac ordered. "Follow her."

"It's five o'clock in the afternoon. The middle of rush hour. How is Talbott supposed to get to her while she's in her car, in the middle of a traffic jam?"

"The same way he got to her in the parking lot at the station. Damn it, Jake! Turn the car around!"

"Man, you're as touchy as a bull with a boil." But he threw on the siren and the lights and swung the car around.

Mac watched the cars scatter in front of them. When he caught sight of A.J.'s car, he said, "There she is."

Jake switched off the lights and siren and they followed A.J. for another mile or two into an increasingly downbeat part of the city. She was several blocks ahead of them, but they saw her pull over near a small row of storefronts, tucked into the end of a block of tall houses.

Just then a truck pulled out in front of them, blocking the street. By the time the truck moved and they reached A.J.'s car, she was nowhere in sight. Mac leaped out of the car, then scanned the street, feeling helpless. Where would she have gone?

Maybe Jake was right. Maybe he was an idiot for following her.

It was for her own good, he reminded himself. If she was too careless to look after herself, someone had to do it for her.

"Want me to park?" Jake asked through the open window of the car.

"No, thanks. I'll find her. She can't be far."

"Then I'm heading back to the station. Give me a yell if you need me."

"Thanks." Mac raised his hand in farewell but didn't look at his partner. He headed for the cluster of shops, hoping that's where she'd gone.

The corner store was a market, the kind that used to exist on every street corner in the city but now were only found in the poor areas of town. Next to it was a Laundromat, a martial-arts academy and a beauty shop.

She wasn't in the market. The Laundromat and beauty parlor were open to view, with big picture windows behind burglar bars. That left the martial-arts school.

He stood outside the door, hesitating. She'd probably be mad as hell he'd followed her. *Too bad.* He pushed open the door.

There was a tiny desk crammed into a narrow hallway just inside. Magazines and books cluttered its surface, and on the wall behind the desk hung an array of plaques and ribbons in a rainbow of colors. A display case next to the desk held trophies, some of them huge.

There were two doors leading off the hallway. He opened one and saw that it led to an empty locker room. The smell of sweat and old gym socks lingered in the air.

He closed the door and reached for the other one. It opened into a large room lined with mirrors. The floor was covered with blue mats. Two people in white uniforms circled each other, feinting, looking for an opening.

One of them was A.J.

Suddenly the man jumped and kicked, looking as if he'd connect with the side of A.J.'s head. She ducked before launching herself at the now unbalanced man. In moments he was on the mat, A.J.'s foot on his neck.

But just when Mac began to breathe again, the man flipped A.J. Mac felt the floor vibrate beneath his feet when she landed. She scrambled to her feet and attacked the man again.

Mac lowered himself to the floor to watch.

CHAPTER TWELVE

A.J. AND HER OPPONENT fought viciously, attacking and feinting, kicking and punching. After every blow she received, she attacked with more determination.

After a half hour, her dark hair was damp with sweat and the back of her uniform was soaked. Her chest rose and fell rapidly beneath the white jacket, and as she backed away from her opponent, she reached down and tightened the dark belt around her waist.

After landing one particularly hard blow, her opponent stopped, crossed his arms over his chest and nodded to her. *Thank God,* Mac thought. Although it looked as though A.J. gave as good as she got, she'd still taken a beating.

"You were stabbed a short time ago. Are you sure you want to practice throws?" the man asked.

"I'm fine," A.J. answered, brushing her hand over her side.

A.J. bowed before walking to the other side of the room. Shrugging off the thin jacket she wore, she picked up a thicker one and slipped it on over her black sports bra. Then she returned to the center of the room.

For the next half hour her opponent came at her from every possible direction. His intent was clear—he wanted to hurt her. A.J. twisted, turned and flipped him onto his back and abdomen. It was a brutal ritual, accompanied by grunts, whistling exhalations of air and A.J.'s low growls. A.J. occasionally landed on the floor, but she put her opponent on the mat more often.

The last time the man landed on the floor, he lay still for a long moment. Then he stood up and placed his hands together, as if he were praying. A.J. immediately followed suit. They bowed to each other, then the man put his arms around A.J. and held her close.

Jealousy rose up inside Mac as he watched A.J. hug her opponent. Recognizing the emotion, unable to banish it, he scowled.

A.J. finally broke free and pushed her damp hair away from her face. "Thank you, Kwan."

"You did well, A.J." He touched one of the bruises on her throat. "Next time you are attacked, you will prevail."

"I would have prevailed this time," she said, her voice wry. "I was distracted and not paying attention."

The man studied her for a moment, then a slight smile curved his mouth. "I think maybe it's good for you to be distracted." He glanced over at Mac, then back at her. "I'll leave you to your cooldown."

A.J.'s opponent walked out of the room and the door closed with a quiet whoosh behind him. Silence settled over the space again.

A.J. closed her eyes and began to move. Her body flowed from one pose to the next, fluid and graceful. The movements were like an elaborate dance, smooth and elegant. And just as seductive.

Finally she stopped. She drew in a deep breath, let it out, then walked over to stand in front of Mac. He scrambled uncomfortably to his feet.

"What are you doing here?" she asked.

"What does it look like? I'm watching you."

"How did you find me?"

He scowled, irritated with his body's response to her. "I followed your car, which wasn't easy considering you were driving like a bat out of hell."

"Why?" She frowned. "Did something happen? Is there a problem?"

"No. The only problem is a strange aversion on my part to seeing you lying bloody on the ground again."

She picked up a bottle of water from the floor and took a drink. "You weren't around," she said stiffly. "And I had an appointment."

He leaned against the wall and watched her face. "That was quite the display you put on."

"I wasn't putting on a display. I was practicing."

"I'm impressed."

She used her palm to slap the water bottle's cap closed. "When Doak attacked me, I let him control me. I should have taken him down. So obviously I need practice."

"You told your buddy that you were distracted that night," he said. "What distracted you?"

Color, which had begun to fade from her cheeks, flooded back. She shrugged without meeting his eyes. "Work, of course."

"Does anything besides work distract you, A.J.?"

Slowly she met his gaze. The distant blare of a car horn on the street seeped into the quiet of the room and a door slammed close by.

Breaking contact, she stooped to pick up the towel on the mat and wiped it across her face and head. Her hair was damp and wildly disordered. The same way it would look, he thought, when she was in bed with a lover.

"I need to go," she said. "Do you want to follow me?"

"Nope."

When she shot him a startled look, he pushed away from the wall. "I need to bum a ride. Can you take me back to the station to pick up my truck?"

"How did you get here?"

"Jake dropped me off." Remembering how they'd charged across traffic to follow her, he dropped his gaze.

She watched him, her eyes measuring. After a moment she said, "Sure. Let's go."

She retrieved the white jacket she'd dropped, then led the way through the door to the tiny reception area.

Her opponent was sitting behind the desk. "I'll be right back," she said, disappearing into the locker room.

"I am Kwan Soo Kim," the man said, extending his hand. "Welcome to my school."

"Thanks." The guy's hand felt like a piece of leather, and his grip was firm and tight. "Mac McDougal."

"You are a friend of A.J.?" he asked delicately.

"We work together."

Dark eyes bored into his, assessing him. Kwan nodded as if satisfied at what he'd seen. "If you are going to distract her, you must also protect her."

"I'm doing my best."

He nodded slowly. "A.J. is good," he said. "She is fast and tough and smart. But her skills won't help if she's not paying attention."

"I'll keep that in mind."

The door to the locker room opened and A.J. slipped out. She carried a bag and wore a pair of bike shorts and a T-shirt. He jerked his gaze away from her thighs and hips, sleek and smoothly muscled, gloved in black. "Ready?" she said. She looked from him to Kwan then back again, a question in her eyes.

"Let's go."

They walked out the door into the shimmering heat of early evening. A.J. unlocked the passenger door of the small sports car, then walked around and slid in the driver's seat.

The interior gleamed. The rich scent of leather surrounded him as he sank down into the seat. When she started the car, the engine purred with restrained power.

"Nice ride."

"I like it." She shifted smoothly into gear and merged into traffic.

She drove fast but not recklessly, shifting from one gear to the next, resting her hand on the gearshift.

"I've been wondering about this car," he said.

She spared him a quick glance. "Wondering what?"

"This doesn't seem like your kind of wheels."

"No?" A tiny smile hovered around her mouth. "What kind of car did you think I drove?"

"Something more predictable. Something more down-to-earth, more practical."

Her smile widened. "That's how you see me? As practical and down-to-earth?"

"I sure as hell don't see you as Mario Andretti."

"I don't exceed the speed limit," she said primly. "I wouldn't dream of speeding, Detective. I'm a law-abiding citizen."

Her wicked grin hit him in the chest like a sledgehammer. "Oh, yeah," he said with feeling. "You have the potential to be a very naughty girl, A.J. I like that about you."

She laughed as she made a right. "You sweet-talker, you. You're just flattering me because you want to drive my car."

He watched as she maneuvered the car smoothly

through the still-crowded streets. "You surprise me," he said quietly. "I don't know what to expect from you."

"Really? You must think I'm pretty predictable at work. We always fight about the same things."

"I'm not talking about work. I'm talking about you. This car. The stuff you were doing today." The open, unapologetic way she'd responded to him. The way she fired his blood, made him ache with hunger.

She shrugged, then shot him a glance. "There's more to you than your job, too, Mac."

"You were impressive back there. You're very skilled."

"Thank you."

"Which discipline was that?"

"Mostly tae kwon do. The throws are judo."

"You're a black belt, aren't you?" He remembered the dark belt cinched at her waist. "What degree?"

"Third degree in tae kwon do. First in judo."

"How long have you been studying?"

"Fourteen years. I started when I was fifteen."

"Martial arts aren't typical activities for fifteen-year-old girls."

"I wanted to be able to defend myself."

"That was more than self-defense I saw today. You were training to seriously hurt someone."

"If I couldn't hurt an attacker, I couldn't defend myself very well, could I?"

He hooked an arm across the back of the seat. "Fifteen-year-old girls think they're invincible. Why did you need self-defense lessons?"

"It's a big, bad world out there," she said. The light they'd stopped at turned green and the car surged forward, "I like to be prepared."

Before he could answer, his cell phone chirped in his pocket. When he saw Jake's number, he flipped it open.

"McDougal."

"Jake here, Mac. You need to meet me at the Danford Woods Forest Preserve. That's the one at the edge of the campus. The university cops have a body at the bottom of a ravine."

"Tripp?"

"Possibly. That's why they called."

"I'm still with A.J. I'll meet you there." He glanced over at A.J. "If it's what you think it is, I'll have one of the patrol guys take her home and stay with her."

"See you." Jake ended the call.

A.J. watched Mac snap his phone closed. His face had changed during the call. He was no longer the man who'd come into the academy and watched her, the man who teased her about her car. He'd become a cop again. His eyes were cold and hard, his face expressionless.

"I need to go to Danford Woods, next to the university. Can you take me?"

"Of course."

Even his voice had changed. There was no softness in him now, no smile.

"What happened?"

For a moment she didn't think he'd answer. But he did. "Someone found a body in a ravine there."

"The missing waitress?"

"Maybe." Tension hummed from his body, a restless energy that could hardly be contained in the small space of her car.

"Are you sure you don't want to get your car?"

"No. Jake is there." He turned to look at her. "I'm going to send you home with a patrol officer. I want you to stay put tonight."

"Sorry, Mac. I have plans."

His face darkened. "Cancel them."

Her hackles rose at his overbearing tone. "That's not an option," she said, her voice cool. "But since I'll be at a restaurant with a friend, I should be safe."

"What do you mean, you'll be at a restaurant with a friend? Do you have a date?"

"I'll pretend you didn't ask me that." She made a left turn into the forest preserve entrance and slowed. "Where should I go?"

"Follow the road. It will be obvious."

She drove down the narrow, winding road, through the dappled shadows cast by trees on either side of them. She rolled down the car window, enjoying the organic smell of earth and plants. The air was noticeably cooler here. The Cook County forest preserves were welcome oases of woods and meadows in Chicago and the surrounding suburbs. Today, apparently, one of them had become a crime scene.

Mac didn't say a word, but she felt him watching her. In spite of the open window, the air in the car was scarce and she couldn't seem to draw enough oxygen into her lungs.

She exhaled in relief when she saw the police cars and ambulance in front of her. She braked and turned to Mac.

"Looks like this is the end of the line," she said, trying to lighten her voice.

"Don't count on it, Ferguson," he said.

He skimmed his hand over her bare thigh, pausing at the edge of her shorts. She couldn't control the tiny shiver that ran up her leg.

"You wearing these on your hot date?" he asked, slipping the tip of his finger under her shorts and slowly running it around the cuff. Desire surged through her. When she sucked in a shocked breath, satisfaction filled his eyes.

"I never did learn how to share," he whispered. "I don't plan on starting now." He moved his hand away, so slowly that she thought she could feel every ridge on his fingertip. Then he hooked his hand around her neck, pulled her close.

His kiss was hard and thorough, and she was shaking when he drew away.

"Something to think about during dinner," he said.

Then he slid out of the car and walked away without looking back.

CHAPTER THIRTEEN

A.J. PULLED INTO the restaurant parking lot and steered to the spot closest to the streetlight, then watched the patrol car drive in behind her.

Mac had ignored her protests and ordered one of the police officers to stay with her the rest of the evening. She locked her door as she watched him park.

The skirt she'd pulled over her bike shorts fluttered around her legs as she strolled to her car. She waited until he rolled down the window. "Thank you, Officer Hightower," she said. "I appreciate you watching out for me."

"No problem, Ms. Ferguson."

The young officer wasn't someone she knew; he looked like he was barely more than a rookie. The boy gave her an earnest smile and started to get out of the car. "I'll wait for you in the bar."

"That's not necessary," she said with a smile. "Nothing's going to happen to me in a restaurant."

"Detective McDougal was very specific," he said. "He told me not to let you out of my sight."

Her smile disappeared. "Is that right?"

"He was worried about you, Ms. Ferguson."

"I'll just bet he was," she said, remembering Mac's questions about her date. Her hand tightened on the car door, holding it shut. "You'll wait for me right here." She gave him a stern look. "I don't want you in the restaurant, watching me. Do you understand?"

"But Detective McDougal said—"

"I don't care what McDougal said. Doak Talbott is not going to assault me in front of a hundred witnesses. You'll be able to see me walk in the door and walk out again, and that's all you need to do. Is that clear?"

The young officer sank down into the seat. "Yes, ma'am. I'll stay right here."

"Good." A.J. stood up. "I'll see you later, then."

"I'll be here when you come out," he assured her.

"Thank you, Officer," she said, relaxing into a smile. "I appreciate that."

She felt the kid cop watching her as she headed for the door, then forgot about him when she stepped into the restaurant and saw her "date."

"A.J."

A slender middle-aged woman enveloped her in a hug. A.J. wrapped her arms around the woman who'd adopted her twelve years earlier. "Kate. I'm so glad to see you."

Kate Ferguson released her, holding onto her hands. She frowned as she studied the bruises on A.J.'s neck. "Those are a lot worse than you led me to believe."

A.J. shrugged. "They don't hurt anymore." She touched Kate's hair, which was cut short and full of highlights. "I like the new look." She grinned. "I bet Frank thinks it's hot."

Kate rolled her eyes, but her face softened into a smile. "All indications are that he likes it."

The maître d' seated them and a waiter came over to their table immediately. "Hi, ladies. The usual tonight?"

"Please," Kate said, and A.J. nodded. When he brought them two glasses of wine a few minutes later, they ordered their meals without looking at the menu.

A.J. took a sip of wine and asked, "How is Frank?"

She was delighted to see the other woman blush. "He's wonderful," Kate answered, her voice endearingly girlish.

"Tell me what you've been up to," A.J. said.

They talked through the meal, catching up on their jobs and mutual friends, until the waiter brought their coffee, and Kate leaned toward A.J.

"What is it, honey?" she asked. "What's bothering you?"

"Is it that obvious?" A.J. ran her finger around the edge of her coffee cup.

"It is to me."

A.J. sighed. "It's a man."

Kate's face lit up. "It's about time."

"It's not that simple. He's a cop."

A knowing smile crept over Kate's face. "It's Mac McDougal, isn't it?"

"How did you know?" A.J. stared at her, astonished.

"You talked about him with such passion. I knew there was something between you."

"I thought the only thing between us was mutual loathing." She turned the coffee cup in its saucer, then looked up to meet Kate's eyes. "Apparently I was wrong."

"Have you slept with him?"

"No." A.J.'s face flared with heat as coffee sloshed out of her cup. "But it took everything I had to say no."

"Why would you even think of saying no?" Kate asked, reaching across the table for her hand.

"You know why."

"A.J., that was fourteen years ago. You were a child. You're a completely different person now."

"I'm a…"

Before she could finish, Kate put her fingers across A.J.'s mouth. "Don't say that. Don't ever say that. It's not true and you know it."

"It *is* true," A.J. said quietly. "No matter what you call it. And Mac is a cop."

She studied her hands, surprised to see them shaking. "I'm afraid that if I tell him what happened, he'll look at me in a different way. Like I was one of 'them,' one of the scumbags they deal with every day. Just like the cops fourteen years ago did." She lifted her head to look at Kate, who was a blur on the other side of the table. "I couldn't bear it."

Kate grasped both of A.J.'s hands in hers. "Listen to me, sweetheart. When we signed those papers twelve years ago, you became my daughter. In every possible way. I couldn't love you more if I had carried you in my body for nine months."

A.J. tightened her grip on Kate's hands as a lump swelled in her throat. "You know I feel the same."

"One of the things we promised that day was that we'd always be straight with each other. We'd always tell the truth, no matter how much it hurt. So you can trust what I say. It's what I believe with all my heart." She leaned closer. "If Mac is any kind of a man, if he cares about you, what happened fourteen years ago isn't going to matter to him."

"Maybe it matters to me," A.J. murmured.

Kate sighed. "I thought you'd gotten past the guilt."

"I have. Mostly. But Mac is different." A.J. moved her spoon around on the saucer, drawing patterns in the spilled coffee. "I'm afraid to tell him. He's important, Kate. And it scares me."

"That just means you're an intelligent woman. When a man is important to you, when he matters, it's supposed to scare you."

"Yeah, well it's hard to get any work done when I'm not sleeping at night."

Kate's lips twitched. "It sounds as if you've gone past scared and right into terrified."

"Are you scared about Frank?"

"I'm petrified with fear," Kate answered. "And he is, too." She touched the back of A.J.'s hand, then sat up straight and reached for the check. "You always did think too much, A.J. It's time you started to feel, as well." A smile spread across her face. "I bet Detective McDougal is having some sleepless nights, too. Maybe the two of you could figure out a way to solve that problem."

A.J. smiled a little as she fiddled with the bag containing the meal she'd ordered for Officer Hightower. "Are mothers really supposed to encourage their daughters to have sex?"

Kate set down her glass of wine. "Mothers want their daughters to be happy. That's all I want for you, A.J. I see a light in your eyes when you talk about Mac, a light I've never seen before. Let yourself be happy, honey. You deserve it."

Before A.J. could answer, a tall bear of a man walked up to the table. "Everyone in this place is going to be jealous when I leave with the two most gorgeous women in the room."

Kate's face lit up. "Hi, Frank."

A matching light filled Frank's eyes. "Hi, baby." He turned to A.J., gave her a kiss. "How's my daughter-to-be?"

"I'm fine."

"Frank, could you follow A.J. home?" Kate asked. "She's having a problem with a client, and the police don't want her to be alone."

"Of course." He gave Kate a lingering kiss. "I'll see you in a little while."

"It's all right, Frank. There's a police officer waiting outside for me. You go on home with Kate," A.J. said.

"Don't be silly. Let the police officer go back to work. I'd love to take you home," Frank replied.

A.J. rose from the table and embraced Kate tightly, drawing comfort from the only mother she'd ever truly had.

"Remember that I love you," Kate whispered.

A.J. walked out the door with Frank, wrapped her arm around his waist and gave him a hug. "Thank you for making her so happy."

"I'd die for Kate," he said quietly. "She's the best thing that ever happened to me." He squeezed her shoulders, smiled down at her. "You need to find someone who makes you just as happy."

A.J. pressed a kiss to his cheek. "People in love become such matchmakers."

"Kate worries about you," Frank said.

"That's what mothers are supposed to do," she said. "Just don't let her start hinting about grandchildren."

They both laughed as they approached Officer Hightower's car. The young officer rolled down the window.

"Thanks for waiting, Officer," she said, handing him the bag. "I thought you might be getting hungry."

"Thank you, Ms. Ferguson," he said fervently. "I am."

"I'm going home now and Frank will follow me," A.J. said. "He'll walk me into my apartment. You probably need to get back to the crime scene at Danford Woods."

"Are you sure?" Hightower looked from her to Frank, uncertainty in his eyes. "Detective McDougal told me to make sure you got home."

"Frank can do that," she said. "Thanks for waiting."

"You bet."

MAC STOOD SEVERAL FEET AWAY from the body sprawled facedown on the rocky ground at the bottom of the ravine, watching the medical examiner work. The doctor had already covered the woman's hands with paper bags, and her assistant was snapping pictures. They didn't have a positive ID yet, but his gut told him it was Helena Tripp.

If only he'd been able to arrest Doak Talbott when Tripp had first been reported missing. The taste of failure was bitter as he watched the too-familiar steps of a homicide investigation. He'd find Doak, he silently promised the murdered woman. No matter how long it took.

"Hey, Detective, what do you need me to do?"

The voice came from behind him, and Mac turned to look at Officer Hightower. His eyes narrowed. "I already gave you an assignment. You were supposed to watch Ms. Ferguson." He jerked his head at the body on the ground. "To keep Doak Talbott from doing that to her."

"I stayed with her at the restaurant," Hightower protested. "But she said the guy she was with would take her home."

"The guy she was with?"

"Yeah, some old dude. The fatherly type."

"Did she say who it was?"

"Nah. She called him Frank."

"Hey, Mac, did you crash and burn with Ferguson?" one of the other officers asked. "What happened to the McDougal touch?"

"We're talking about Ferguson," another officer, Lewis, reminded him. "She's so cold she'd give the devil frostbite."

"Why don't you morons pay attention to what we're doing here?" Mac snarled, trying to ignore the pain in his chest. "Even dipsticks like you might learn something."

Lewis laughed, and Mac stared at the body of Helena Tripp. Jealousy dripped like acid against his heart, making it burn.

Making him ache.

He shoved his hands into his pockets. This was why he didn't get serious with any of the women he dated. This was why he always left first. He didn't need any more reminders of what he lacked. He knew they would eventually look inside him and see nothing but a gaping hole.

Damn A.J.'s beeper. If it hadn't interrupted them the night before, they would have made love. She would be his, bonded to him. At least for a while, until she learned the truth about him.

Lust, pain and loss twisted together. Tonight, he promised. He'd make her his tonight.

A.J. LEANED AGAINST THE CLOSED DOOR to her apartment, the smile fading from her face as she listened to Frank hurrying away. Back to Kate. Kate and Frank acted like the luckiest people in the world, and she loved them both too much to be envious.

But an ember of jealousy burned inside her.

Mac's face drifted into her mind, and she let it linger there. Could she and Mac eventually have what Kate and Frank shared? Was he a man she could love?

The answer came far too readily. No man had ever dominated her thoughts the way he did. She'd never found a man so fascinating on so many levels.

She'd never wanted a man the way she wanted Mac.

Throwing on the boxers and T-shirt she used as pajamas, she curled up on the couch and picked up the mystery she'd been reading. But her mind kept wandering to Mac, wondering what he was doing, wondering about the body they'd found. Realizing reading was futile, she snapped the book shut and turned on the television.

Two hours later there was a knock on her door. She

leaped to her feet, her heart pounding. There was only one person who'd come to her door this late at night.

"Who's there?" she asked. But she knew.

"Mac."

"Hold on a moment."

She raced into the bedroom and grabbed a robe, shoving her arms into it as she hurried back to the door.

"Come on in," she said, opening the door.

His eyes held a hint of uncertainty she'd never seen in Mac before. "Were you busy, A.J.? Did I interrupt you?"

"Not at all." Studying him, she saw the strain around his eyes, the tightness of his mouth. She moved aside so he could enter the apartment.

"I was putting on my robe," she said.

His gaze skimmed over her and the uncertainty became desire. "That wasn't necessary," he said. "Not for me."

"Especially for you." She pushed Kate's words out of her mind. "Sit down. Do you want coffee? Or a beer?"

"No. I don't want anything to drink."

"What do you want?" Her heart beat heavily against her ribs.

He hooked a finger in the collar of her T-shirt and tugged, drawing her slowly toward him.

"You, A.J. I want you."

She took a step closer, then another.

A fraction of an inch separated them when he released her T-shirt. Need had turned his eyes a dark, midnight blue. "I can't get you out of my head, A.J. I can't think of anything but you."

He let his hand trail down the front of her robe, and hunger leaped inside her. She swayed closer to him, felt her breasts brush against his chest. He smoothed his thumbs lightly over her lips. "Mac," she whispered before melting against him. He moved forward and she stumbled with him, until her back was pressed against the wall.

"I'm going to be the only one in your head, A.J. The next time you have a date, you won't be able to think of anyone but me."

"A date?" she managed to say. "What are you talking about?"

Instead of answering he bent closer, until his mouth was barely brushing hers. "Did he taste you like this?" he whispered, touching his tongue to her lips.

She shivered. One touch, and she was helpless in his arms.

"Did he know how to kiss you?"

His tongue mimicked the movements of his hips against her, and she struggled to draw herself back from the cliff edge. "Who are you talking about?"

"Your date tonight. Did he touch you like this?" He slid his hand beneath her T-shirt, stroking her abdomen, drifting closer to her breast. She moved restlessly, needing his touch, aching for it. When he cupped his hand around her breast, she shuddered against him.

"I didn't…" She needed to stop, she told herself dimly. She needed to find out what Mac was talking about. But reason was fading, being replaced with an all-consuming need for him.

He tugged at her robe, pulling it apart. Then he shoved her T-shirt up. Dazed, she heard the sound of material ripping. For a moment he stood still, staring down at her. Then he bent and took her nipple in his mouth, causing her to make a tiny, keening sound in the back of her throat.

He lifted his head, his eyes glittering. "Did he want you as much as I do?"

Only his body pressed against hers kept her upright. She would have fallen if he'd moved away.

He brought his hands back to her face, caressing her lightly as if he were trying to memorize her by touch alone. But when she moaned and reached for him, his kiss wasn't gentle. It dominated, demanding submission. Claiming her.

And she surrendered completely. Nothing else mattered. She was desperate to have him.

She reached for the waist of his jeans, her hand unsteady as she unbuttoned them. Then she shoved his jeans down his legs, held him between her hands.

He jerked against her, his mouth devouring hers. His hands pulled her boxers down her legs. Then he slid his fingers into her and found her wet. He groaned against her mouth.

He kicked away his jeans and slid a condom into place. Then he lifted her legs around his waist and entered her. A cry of shocked pleasure escaped from her mouth. She locked her legs around him and held on while he thrust into her. The sound of her body hitting into the wall reverberated in her head.

"You're mine, A.J." His breath was hot in her ear.

She soared higher and higher, tiny cries erupting from her throat, until release exploded through her. "Mac," she sobbed, barely able to hold onto him, helpless against the violent contractions of her body.

He followed her moments later, his cry muffled against her mouth.

She had no idea how long they stood there, his body pressing hers into the wall, holding her up. Eventually he lifted his head and eased away from her.

He gathered the shredded remnants of her T-shirt, clutching them together in his fist. Staring down at her, he touched the stinging whisker burn on her neck, the red marks next to her breast, her swollen lips. "A.J.," he whispered. "What did I do to you?"

CHAPTER FOURTEEN

"WHAT DID YOU DO?" She kissed him, burrowing her hands beneath his shirt to touch his back. "You turned me inside out." She smiled against his mouth. "You made the earth move. I'm pretty sure the sun and moon moved, too."

His hands trembled where he held her T-shirt together, then he grasped her arms and stepped away from her. Instead of the tenderness she expected to see on his face, there was only shame.

"Mac?" She couldn't keep the uncertainty from her voice. "What's wrong?"

"I didn't mean for this to happen," he said without meeting her gaze.

"What?" Ice crept into her veins. "You said…" *You said you needed me.*

"I said a lot of things when I got here tonight that I shouldn't have said."

She slid away from him and straightened her robe. Her hands shook and humiliation swept through her in a hot, mortifying wave.

"Then I guess you should leave," she managed to say. Pain enveloped her. It was all around her, throbbing like a living thing, until it was the only thing she could feel or see.

He finally met her gaze. "Not yet. I'm sorry, A.J."

She shrugged as if her heart weren't breaking, refusing to let him see how he'd devastated her. "What for? You didn't hear me telling you to stop, did you? You're the one who said last night that we're both adults. You screwed me, it was fun, goodbye."

"I didn't want to 'screw' you."

"Then you get an Oscar," she said, her voice flat. "Because that was a world-class performance."

"Can we talk about this?" he said.

"You want a play-by-play analysis?" Her hands tightened on the belt of her robe. "Fine. Ripping my T-shirt was a little over the top. Everything else? No complaints."

He flushed. "That's not what I meant."

"Then what do you want to talk about? Feelings?" She raised her eyebrows, knowing she was hurting him, too full of pain to hold the words back. "I thought Mac McDougal didn't do feelings."

"There are a lot of things I thought I didn't do." His gaze wandered to the wall and his mouth tightened. "I was wrong."

Her throat swelled with tears, overflowed into her eyes. "I want you to leave," she said. She would *not* cry in front of him. It would just complete the evening's humiliation.

"Not until I say what I need to say." He reached for her hands, but she yanked them away. "I was angry and hurt when I walked in the door. And I dealt with it in the worst possible way."

"Why were you angry and hurt?"

"I was angry about the body we found. Angry that a young woman was dead. And I was hurt that you'd been on a date. Angry that you were with another man."

"Hold on." She vaguely remembering him talking about a date just before he'd… She pulled the lapels of her robe together, sickness rising inside her. "What do you mean, 'I was on a date'?"

"Tonight. At the restaurant. Your date."

"I met someone for dinner. Why did you think it was a date?"

"I asked you about your date and you didn't deny it. Then Hightower told me who you were with. Who took you home."

"Hightower?" Anger nudged at the hurt and confusion. She welcomed it. "Officer Hightower said I was on a date?"

"He saw you hugging the guy when you came out of the restaurant."

She stared at him in disbelief for a moment. Then she pushed past him, her hands curling into fists. "You thought I was on a date?"

He shoved his hand through his hair. "You're making me crazy. When you said you were meeting someone, all I could think about was some guy seeing you in the tight black shorts you were wearing. All I could think about was some guy peeling them off you. And all I wanted to do was peel them off you myself."

"You actually thought I had a date with another man?"

"What was I supposed to think?"

"Exactly what I told you. That I was meeting a friend for dinner."

"I told you, A.J. You're making me crazy," he muttered.

"Last night I almost made love with you on this couch," she said, her hand gesturing toward it. "If my beeper hadn't gone off, we would have made love. And you think that tonight I'm off on a date with another man? Is that the kind of woman you think I am?"

"Of course not," he muttered. "And think is the key word. I didn't think. I just reacted."

"Fine. You can just think yourself out of my house. And take your reactions with you."

She stormed past him and flung open her door. Cool air from the hall drifted in and she shivered. She would never be warm again.

Mac scrubbed a hand over his face. "I won't leave like this. With you angry. And hurt."

"Now you're concerned about my feelings?" It took every ounce of strength she possessed to give him a cool look. "I might have believed that if you hadn't assumed I was a woman with a string of lovers."

He flinched. "You don't pull your punches, do you?"

"Why would I? To spare your feelings?"

"I deserve that," he said grimly. "I deserve everything you throw at me. But don't shut me out. Don't throw away what we have here."

" 'What we have'?" Her voice was flat. "We have hot sex and that's it. I've got news for you, ace. Hot sex just to scratch an itch isn't very hot. In fact, it's downright cold. And I'm not interested in it."

"You were pretty interested a few minutes ago," he said, and she saw the beginnings of anger on his face.

She was glad to see it. It would hold back the tears, at least for a little while. "That was before I knew what you thought of me. That was when I thought there was more between us than hormones."

He closed his eyes for a long moment. When he opened them, the anger was gone, replaced by a softness she didn't want to see. "A.J.," he said, his voice intimate in the late-night stillness. "You know there's more between us than sex."

He cupped his hand around her face and for one traitorous second, she wanted to lean into it, into the comfort he offered.

She jerked her head away. "Get out, Mac."

He took his hand away, but he didn't move. "You think I'm going to leave? That I'm going to forget about this, pretend it never happened? Not going to happen, A.J. I won't forget how you felt in my arms. I won't forget how you moaned my name when I touched you. I won't forget anything."

She turned away from him, blinking furiously, trying to stop the tears from spilling out of her eyes. "Leave," she whispered.

She felt him behind her, prayed he wouldn't touch her.

"Please don't cry," he whispered, turning her around, enveloping her in his arms. "Yell at me, throw something at me, toss me on the floor. But don't cry. I can bear anything but your tears."

"I'm not crying," she said fiercely. "I never cry."

Tears welled up in her eyes again, and she stepped out of his embrace, used both hands to shove him out the door. As he stumbled backward, off balance, she slammed the door behind him. The dead bolt slid into place with the lonely ring of finality.

"A.J., let me in," he said against the door. "Please. I won't leave like this."

She sank to the floor, pressing her hands over her ears to shut out the sound of his voice, and let the tears fall.

MAC WAS LATE GETTING TO WORK the next morning. He threw himself into his chair, sick at heart and on edge. He wanted to fight with A.J. A fight would clear the air.

"Hey, partner. Nice to see you could make it."

He'd settle for a fight with Jake.

"Up yours, Donovan."

Jake strolled over, studying him. "Hell's bells, son. You look like something dragged backward through a cat door."

"Nice to see your cheerful face this morning, too."

The teasing smile disappeared from Jake's face. "What's wrong?" he asked quietly. "What happened?"

"We found Helena Tripp's body yesterday. Or did that slip your mind?"

"Helena Tripp didn't put that hurt on your face."

Mac involuntarily glanced at the closed door to A.J.'s office. "Drop it, Jake."

"Let's go get some coffee," Jake said after a moment. "You look like you need a big one, and the stuff in here is more vile than usual this morning."

Before Mac could refuse, Jake had him down the stairs and out the door. As soon as Jake's pickup truck was out of the lot, he said, "What is it, partner?"

Mac stared out the window. After a moment he turned to Jake. "Was she in her office?"

"Came in just a little before you did." Jake didn't even bother to pretend he didn't know who Mac was asking about. "She looked about as bad as you do. What I could see of her, anyway."

"What do you mean, 'what you could see of her'?"

Mac clenched his fists. "Was she hurt? I called patrol to follow her in. Did something happen to her?"

"Whoa, partner." The look Jake gave him was laced with pity. "All I meant was that she had sunglasses on."

"Then what do you mean, she looked bad?"

"She looked drained." He shot a speculative look at Mac. "You keep her up all night?"

"Only in my dreams," Mac said bitterly.

Jake pulled to a stop in front of a Starbucks, then leaned against the door. "You're my partner and A.J.'s my friend. You want to talk about it?"

"I screwed up," he said. "I really screwed up. She threw me out and wouldn't even talk to me."

"The love train derailed?" Jake shook his head. "There's only one thing a man can do when that happens. Crawl. Crawl like a dog and beg her to forgive you."

Mac smothered a painful laugh. "She won't let me close enough to crawl."

"What the hell did you do to her?" All trace of teasing was gone from Jake's voice.

"I accused her of cheating on me."

"A.J.? You accused A.J. of cheating on you?" Jake's face darkened "The last thing that woman would do is cheat on a lover. Are you clear on that?" Jake's glare punched Mac in the face.

"I know." Mac rubbed his hand across his face, but it only triggered more memories. When he'd shaved that morning, he'd remembered what it had felt like to rub his face over A.J.'s soft skin. He'd left marks on her, red whisker burns. He wanted to kiss them away.

"I know she wouldn't cheat." He closed his eyes. "I knew even before I said it."

"Then what the hell got into you?"

Mac stared out the window, watched the people hurry in and out of Starbucks. He wondered if A.J. had stopped here on her way to work.

"I was scared and angry," he said in a low voice. "Angry because of Tripp, angry because we can't find Talbott. But mostly angry with her, because I thought she'd been on a date."

He slumped lower in the seat. "That shook me, Jake. Rocked me sideways. I was so blind with jealousy, so hurt, I couldn't think straight. It scared the hell out of me.

"It's never bothered me before. If a woman I'm seeing wants to see someone else, fine. There's always another woman around the corner. But when I thought A.J. had a date, I lost it."

"I guess the guys ragging on you yesterday at the crime scene didn't help," he said.

"They were just being cops," Mac replied. But his chest ached when he thought about their teasing, and the pain he'd felt.

There was a long beat of silence in the truck before Jake said, "If it makes you feel any better, she looked like hell this morning, too."

"That's supposed to make me feel better? Knowing she's miserable because of me?"

"Would you rather hear that she came in this morning all perky and happy?"

Mac scowled. "A.J. is not perky."

"You know what I mean." Jake got out of the truck and slammed the door, and Mac reluctantly followed him. Inside the shop, espresso machines hissed and customers murmured in low tones. While they waited for their coffee, Jake said, "You're right, Mac. You screwed up royally." He gave Mac a glance full of pity as he picked up his coffee. "And I have no suggestions. A.J. is one stubborn woman when she wants to be."

"You're not telling me anything I don't know."

"I hope you know how to grovel. Because if you want her back, you're going to be doing plenty of it."

He'd never groveled in his life. "Not a problem. I'm a real fast learner."

His mood didn't lighten when he got back to the station. A.J.'s door was open, and moments after he threw himself into his desk chair, she walked out of her office. Accompanying her was a young man he vaguely remembered. The kid was a college student and had been mugged at gunpoint a couple of weeks earlier.

A.J. smiled at the kid, and regret swept over Mac. When he realized he was watching as she walked across the room, he scowled and yanked open a desk drawer. A few moments later, A.J. walked past him on the way to her office, and he pretended to be absorbed in reading a file.

The words were merely a blur of letters, but he stared at it, brooding. He couldn't afford to be distracted. He had to concentrate on Talbott, on finding him before he hurt someone else.

"What are we doing this morning, Jake?" he called to his partner.

"We need to go back to the country club," Jake said. "Also talk to Mindy again. Maybe even the kid."

Mac nodded. "You take the country club this time. I'll go talk to the kid since he knows me. I think he was about to say something last time I was there."

"Sounds good." Jake made a few notes in the file he was reading, then slipped it into a drawer. "I'll catch up with you later."

Mac nodded. When Jake disappeared down the stairs, Mac headed toward A.J.'s office. Her door was open a crack, and he could see her talking on the phone. When she looked up to see him standing there, something flickered in her eyes for a moment, then her face went carefully blank.

When she finished her call, she waved him in.

"Good morning, A.J.," he said.

She examined him for a moment. "Hello, Detective." Her voice held no trace of warmth or welcome. It was as if she were meeting a stranger for the first time, a stranger she found slightly distasteful.

"I'm going to talk to Jamie Talbott," he said, jamming his hands into his pockets. He felt tongue-tied and awkward, like a schoolboy with a crush on the cutest girl in his class. "Do you want to come with me?"

"You can't talk to Jamie today."

"What's wrong? Is he sick?"

"No. But he's in bad shape. He woke up screaming with nightmares several times the last two nights." The sympathy in her eyes warmed her face for a few seconds. "Cissy called me a couple of nights ago to talk about it. I thought you'd want to talk to Jamie again after finding Helena Tripp's body, so I called Cissy this morning."

"You're telling me I can't talk to Jamie." His voice was flat, and he could feel anger rising within him.

"Yes. Cissy was very specific."

"I don't give a damn what Cissy said. That kid is a witness in a murder investigation. He was about to tell me something when I saw him, and I'm going to find out what it was." He put his hands on her desk. "Stay here or come with me. I don't care. But I'm going to see Jamie."

She stared up at him, her eyes cool and impersonal. He was impressed in spite of himself at her control. "You're wasting your time. But in case you talk your way past Cissy, I'll come with you."

She stood up, grabbed her purse and walked around the desk. The skirt she wore was dark blue and ended above her knees. When he found himself staring at her legs, re-membering how they'd felt wrapped around him, he jerked his gaze to her face again. He caught a glimpse of pain in her eyes before she bent to grab a file. When she straightened, her face was composed and unreadable again.

Neither of them spoke as they headed toward the hotel. A.J. kept her gaze focused on the road. The silence in his truck grew thicker, heavier, an awkward presence squatting between them.

"Do you mind if we stop for coffee?" he asked. One cup wasn't going to do it for him today.

"Not at all." She answered without looking at him.

He pulled in front of the same Starbucks he and Jake had visited earlier. She followed him into the store, placed her order and waited in line with him. They might have been total strangers.

Temper stirred inside him as they walked to his truck. He slammed his door with a little too much force, then leaned against it inside and folded his arms.

"Enough with the silent treatment. This isn't high school, A.J. Let's thrash this out right now."

DOAK TALBOTT SNAPPED to attention as he saw the cop and the bitch walk out of the coffee shop. It was the cop who'd come to the house that night. And the bitch who'd been with him, the one he'd almost had at the police station.

Excitement rose inside him. Where were they going? Did it have anything to do with Mindy? Or Jamie?

He smiled with satisfaction. He'd seen her at this coffee shop before. He passed it frequently, hoping she'd come back. As a bonus, she had the cop with her.

Waiting at a stoplight down the street, he watched as they got into an SUV in front of the Starbucks. Perfect. By the time they pulled out, the light would have turned green and he'd slip right in behind them. Who knew where they might take him?

He drove as slowly as he could, but they hadn't moved by the time the light changed. As he passed the black SUV, he saw them talking.

His hands curled into fists. He almost pulled into an empty parking space to wait for them, but he stopped himself in time. The cop would notice. He'd have to go around the block.

By the time he returned to the coffee shop, the SUV was gone. He raced to the corner, but there was no sign of them. They'd gotten away from him.

Rage swelled inside him. He would find the bitch again. And this time, she'd tell him everything she knew. He knew just how to make her do it.

CHAPTER FIFTEEN

A.J. TOOK A SIP of her coffee. It burned all the way to her stomach and continued to eat away at its lining when she looked at Mac. Raising her eyebrows, she managed to keep her voice cool. "I wasn't aware there was anything we needed to thrash out. Do you have a problem with me contacting Cissy?"

"I'm not talking about the damn case and you know it." He ran his hand through his hair in a familiar gesture of frustration. "You're acting like I'm a complete stranger. Damn it, A.J. I said I was sorry. I admitted I'm a total jerk. What more do you want? You want me to crawl? I'll crawl. You want me to take out an ad in the *Herald-Times* and tell the world I'm a jerk, I'll do that, too. Just don't look through me as if I don't exist."

"I'm not having this conversation with you," she said, her chest tightening. "Especially now. I have a job to do and I'm going to do it. Jamie Talbott is all I intend to think about."

An emotion that might have been desperation flickered in his eyes. "Fine. We'll go talk to Jamie. We'll finish working today. Then I'll follow you home and we can talk."

"I'm not going home after work."

He raised his eyebrows. "Ever again? You're moving? Isn't that a little extreme?"

Her eyes narrowed. "Sarcasm doesn't flatter you. I'm going to Kwan's studio." She gave him what she hoped was a cool smile. "I need to work out some aggression."

"Fine. We'll talk after you work out."

"After I work out, I'm going to my yoga class."

"Yoga? After Kwan's?" He stared at her with disbelief. "You beat the crap out of someone, then go meditate about it?"

She turned away from him, suddenly exhausted. "There's no point, Mac. You were a jerk and I was a fool. Let's leave it at that."

"Why were you a fool?"

She looked at him again. "I don't think I need to spell it out for you."

"A.J.," he said, leaning closer. "You're no—"

"Stop," she said sharply. "We're not going to discuss this. We're supposed to be talking to Jamie Talbott."

Their gazes locked on each other as the air in the car seemed to hold its breath. Neither of them moved as the moment stretched longer. Uncomfortable with the resolve in his eyes, she looked away first.

"I'll let you use Jamie as an excuse for now," he said

in a low voice. "But I'm taking you to Kwan's tonight. And your yoga class afterward. And then we'll talk."

He started the car and they headed toward the hotel where Cissy and Jamie hid. Mac's eyes glanced in the rearview mirror every few seconds.

"You're not a fool," he said into the silence.

When she didn't answer, he glanced over at her. "You're a lot of things, A.J., but a fool isn't one of them."

"You made me feel like one," she said, appalled to hear her voice tremble.

"That's the last thing I wanted to do," he said. "I know I hurt you. Humiliated you. I need to know how to fix it."

A sob caught in her throat and she stared blindly out the window. "I don't know."

"You want to punish me, that's okay," he said. "I deserve it. Just tell me I haven't killed everything between us."

"I'm not trying to punish you, Mac. I just don't know how to fix this." She'd never allowed herself to care about a man the way she cared about Mac. And she knew now why she hadn't.

"I'm not going to let this go," he said. "I'm not going to let you walk away from this."

Silence filled the car as he drove through side streets for a while, constantly checking the rearview mirror. They parked a couple of blocks away from the hotel.

The sidewalk was too narrow for her to stay as far away from him as she would have liked. Their shoulders almost brushed several times as they walked along, sending bittersweet longing through her.

When they reached the hotel room, she stood beside him, helpless to ignore him. The knowledge that she wouldn't be able to forget Mac, to put him out of her life easily, suffused her with despair.

Cissy answered Mac's knock almost immediately. "Detective. A.J. What can I do for you?"

"I need to talk to Jamie," Mac said.

Cissy gave A.J. a bewildered look. "I told you this morning that it wouldn't be a good idea."

"I know you did," Mac answered. "Ms. Ferguson was very clear on that. I overruled her." His mouth tightened. "We found the body of a missing young woman yesterday. The last person to see her alive was Doak Talbott. It's urgent that I talk to Jamie."

Cissy glanced from Mac to A.J., then squared her shoulders. "I'm afraid that's not possible right now. I understand your urgency, but Jamie is sleeping. He hasn't slept well recently, and I won't wake him up."

"What time can I come back?" Mac asked.

"I discussed this with A.J."

A.J. put her hand on Cissy's arm. "I'll explain to Mac. But we need to see him soon, Cissy."

Cissy nodded, then closed the door. Mac looked at A.J. "What are you going to explain to me?"

"Let's go, Mac."

Without waiting to see if he followed her, she headed toward the elevator. In a moment she heard him behind her.

Back in the SUV, A.J. said, "Cissy wants to give Jamie another day or two. His nightmares started after you talked to him last time, and she's afraid that they'll get worse if you question him again."

"The best way to get rid of his nightmares is to make sure his father is locked up."

"Cissy knows that. But her first priority is protecting Jamie." She wanted to lean toward Mac, to touch his arm and make him understand. She laced her fingers together instead. "There's only a slim chance that Jamie knows anything. Give him a couple of days to recover."

Mac's jaw worked as he drove. Finally he said, "I'll give him as long as I can. Does that work for you?"

"What works for me doesn't matter," she said. "I hope it works for Jamie."

BY THE TIME A.J. was ready to leave that afternoon and head over to Kwan's studio, her head ached and her stomach hurt. Mac hadn't tried to talk to her again, but every time she'd walked into the bull pen, she'd been aware of his brooding gaze following her. As she slipped out of her office, she was relieved to see him on the phone. She could tell Jake she was leaving and avoid Mac's escort.

She was ashamed of her cowardice, but she couldn't bear to be around Mac. Every time she looked at him, talked to him, another tiny piece of her heart tore away. If she didn't avoid him, there would be nothing left.

"Hey, Jake," she said, stopping by his desk.

He looked up at her with a flashing smile. "Hey yourself, A.J. You taking off?"

She nodded. "Tell Mac I've gone to Kwan's."

"You could wait a few minutes and he'll go with you."

The sympathy in Jake's eyes made her throat tighten. She shook her head. "Not necessary."

"Are you sure?"

"I'm sure."

He stood up. "Then I'll walk you out."

"Thanks."

As they walked, Jake slung an arm over her shoulders. "He's an idiot, but he means well," he said.

She slipped out from under his arm. "What did he say to you?"

"He didn't give me any details, if that's what you're asking. He just said that he'd screwed up."

"Then he got one thing right, at least. Leave it alone, Jake."

"Hey, I'm just looking out for myself," he said. "He was a pain in the rear end today, and I have to work with him."

"He'll get over it."

She felt him looking at her. "You sure about that?"

She didn't know the answer.

They opened the door to bright sunlight and withering heat. "Thanks, Jake," she tossed over her shoulder. "I'll see you tomorrow."

"Be careful, A.J."

AN HOUR AND A HALF LATER, drenched in sweat, her muscles quivering with exhaustion, she bowed to Kwan and murmured the formal words of thanks. When they straightened, her teacher looked at her with speculation.

"You did well today, A.J. Better than last time." He hesitated, then asked delicately, "Is there a reason for your ferocity on the mat?"

She shrugged. "There's a case at work. I needed to work off my frustration."

"I see," he said, his mouth curving into a slight smile as he watched her. "If your frustration continues, come back tomorrow."

"Thanks, Kwan." She picked up her towel and wiped her face, then took a long drink of water. "I will."

An hour later, she walked out of her yoga class into lengthening shadows, dressed in the black spandex shorts she wore under her *dobok* and a loose T-shirt. Guilt nibbled at her. She should have waited for Mac. But he hadn't shown up at Kwan's, and she hadn't wanted to miss her yoga class. She needed its calming influence tonight.

Maybe Mac had decided to listen to her, to stay away. Grief stabbed her, but she pushed it away. She didn't want to think about Mac. She'd stop and pick up a pizza, then go home to shower and relax.

The tiny storefront where she bought her pizza was in a strip mall along a side street. As she pulled into the parking lot, she glanced into her rearview mirror, then studied the cars around her. Nothing looked out of place or threatening. A boy bounced a basketball in the park down the street, cutting around imaginary defenders then leaping into the air to lay the ball in the basket. A woman walked down the sidewalk, towed by a brown-and-white mutt as it tried to smell everything they passed.

The pizza she'd ordered wasn't finished baking, so she chatted with the elderly man behind the counter while she waited. Ten minutes later, she stepped outside into full night, holding the warm cardboard box. The weak glow of the streetlight flickered over the tops of the cars, leaving valleys of gloom between them.

A.J. slowed as she walked toward her car. Maybe she shouldn't have stopped here. Maybe she should have gone straight home while there was still some daylight.

Shaking off her nerves, she slipped her keys into her hand and headed for her car. As she turned the key in the lock, a man stood up in front of her car.

"Don't move."

Doak's eyes glittered in the weak light, and something big and black was in his hand. As she stared at it, he moved closer.

"It's a gun," he said as he slid between her car and the next one. He stood in front of her, a careful arm's length away. "Put the pizza down."

She set it on the roof of her car, along with her purse.

"Now put your hands at your side, like we're having a friendly conversation." He glanced beyond her, and she knew he was trying to see if the owner of the pizza place had noticed him. Apparently whatever he saw satisfied him.

"Where are Mindy and Jamie?" The gun in his hand was steady as a rock.

"I'm not sure. After the fire, they were moved to different shelters. I don't know who went where."

Anger contorted his face. "Don't lie to me, bitch. You were the one who moved them. You know where they are."

"How do you know that?" She kept her eyes fixed on his as she shuffled a fraction of a step closer to him.

"I have my sources." He lifted the gun higher, so it was pointing directly at her heart. "Tell me."

"Why would I do that? You're going to kill me anyway." Another slight movement toward him.

"This gun can cause a lot of pain before it kills you."

She shrugged and slid two inches closer. "I have a high pain tolerance."

"Let's find out." He lowered the gun until it was

pointed at her knee. He looked down to aim, and she flew at him.

The first kick connected with his arm and knocked the gun into the air. The next one caught him square in the chest and sent him staggering backward two steps.

He recovered quickly, but instead of running, he leaped toward her. She let his momentum carry him as she flipped him over and onto the ground. When he tried to scramble up again, she kicked him in the head. He collapsed facedown on the pavement and lay still.

Her cell phone. She needed her cell phone.

Her hand shook as she kept her gaze on Doak and groped for her purse. Mac. She had to get Mac. He would take Doak away, and Jamie and Mindy would be safe.

She would be safe.

Her hand closed around the cell phone in her purse, but it squirted out of her hand and slid beneath the car.

Panic fluttered in her chest. How would she call Mac?

The lights from the pizza restaurant glowed in front of her. She stepped around Doak, staying far enough away that he couldn't grab her, then ran into the store.

"Call 911," she cried.

The owner turned to face her, surprise on his face. "What's wrong?"

"Doak is out there," she said nonsensically. "Call the police!"

"Okay." He kept her in sight as he picked up the phone. His fingers moved with agonizing slowness as he punched in the numbers. Finally he cleared his throat and spoke.

"Yes. There's a woman who says Doak is here," he began. "She told me—"

A.J. reached over the counter and grabbed the phone away from him. Clutching it with shaking hands, she gave the address of the pizza place, then continued, "This is A.J. Ferguson. Send a squad car and contact Detective McDougal. Doak Talbott just attacked me. He's still here, knocked out."

As she listened to the 911 operator's instructions, she turned to look out the window. Doak had disappeared.

"He's gone," she cried, her fingers gripping the phone so tightly they cramped. "Doak is gone!"

"Can you see which way he went?" the voice asked.

"No." She peered into the parking lot but saw no movement. "I don't see him."

"Stay where you are. A squad car will be there soon."

If she ran outside, looked down the street, she might see Doak running away. She might see him get into a car, be able to tell Mac the license plate number. She took a step toward the door, then stopped.

It would be stupid to open that door. The memory of that gun, pointing steadily at her chest, was too vivid in her mind. The horror she'd felt when he lowered it to her knee came surging back, and her legs began to shake.

But it might be their only chance to catch Doak. She pushed the door open and stepped outside, then faltered. She couldn't walk between those cars.

By the time she'd forced herself to move, to walk toward the street, she heard the sirens approaching. Moments later two squad cars raced into the parking lot, one at each end, lights flashing. She heard the siren of another approaching.

"You all right, A.J.?" One of the patrol officers leaped out of the car and ran to her.

"I'm fine. Doak's getting away."

"You sure it was him?"

"I'm sure. Go!"

"You see which way he went?"

"No." Shame rippled through her. "He got away when I wasn't looking."

He nodded once then jumped back into the car. The tires squealed as he peeled out of the lot.

By the time the third squad car pulled up, the officer from the second one had reached her. "Get in my car and sit down," he said. "The paramedics are right behind me."

She shook off his hand. "I'm fine. I don't need the paramedics. The only thing I need is for you to find Doak Talbott." She gestured toward the street. "He couldn't have gotten far. Go look for him."

"There are a couple more cars on the way. Show me what happened."

She pointed out her car, and where Doak had been waiting. As she watched him crouch down and examine the pavement, she realized she was shaking. She wrapped her arms around herself and tried to hold herself still.

"A.J." Strong hands grasped her shoulders and spun her around. Mac towered over her, his face taut with strain. "Are you all right?"

"I'm fine," she said, ashamed to hear her voice wobble. "I'm fine. He never touched me."

He searched her face, his hands gripping her shoulders. Then he closed his eyes and yanked her into his arms, trapping her hands against his chest.

"A.J." He held her so tightly she could barely breathe. She heard his ragged breaths as he buried his face in her hair. When she struggled against him, he eased away from her.

"You're sure you're all right? You're not hurt?" He brushed her hair away from her face, skimmed his hand down her cheek and onto her throat. The bruises from Doak's last attack had faded, but she knew they were still visible. Mac's fingers trembled against her skin.

"Don't," she whispered, reaching up to smooth away the lines of strain on his face. "Don't look like that. Just hold me for a minute, Mac. That's all I need."

He pulled her close again, but this time he cradled her as if she were fine china, delicate and easily crushed. His heart beat beneath her ear, steady and reassuring. His arms warmed her, beating back the chill that reached bone deep. She wrapped her arms around him and held on as if she couldn't bear to let him go.

Finally he eased away from her, but he kept one arm around her shoulders. He led her closer to the building, under the lights. "Tell me what happened," he said.

She took a moment to organize her thoughts, sucked in a deep breath and met his eyes. "It was my fault," she said, swallowing hard.

He looked at her for a long moment without answering. "Yeah, it was," he said. "You should have waited for me."

"I know." Her gaze touched her car, now surrounded by police officers. "But I needed to go to Kwan's studio and you were on the phone and I was…"

"You were mad as hell at me."

She let out a weary sigh. "Yes. I was mad at you. And I did a stupid thing."

"I tried to catch up to you at Kwan's, but you were already gone."

"I was wrong. I'm sorry."

"Now that we've gotten the confessional portion of the story over with, tell me what happened."

She told him slowly, with as much detail as she could remember, exactly what Doak had said and done. Exactly what he wore, and how he looked.

"The son of a bitch is getting desperate," Mac said quietly. "Either Mindy or Jamie knows something."

One of the police officers walked toward them. "Is this your cell phone, A.J.?" he asked.

"Yes," she said, taking it. "I dropped it when I was trying to call 911."

"I have a few questions," the officer began, but Mac stepped between them.

"She already told me how it went down," Mac said. "I'll write the report, and if you have any other questions, you can ask her tomorrow."

The patrol officer looked doubtfully from her to Mac, then shrugged. "Works for me. If you want to write the report, be my guest."

Mac turned to A.J. "Give me your car keys."

She reached for her pocket but her hand skimmed down the side of the tight shorts. "I don't have them. I must have dropped them."

"Find her keys, then drive her car back to her place," Mac ordered the officer. He rattled off her address. "I'm taking her home."

Keeping one arm firmly around her, he walked to her car and snagged her purse and the box of pizza from the roof. "Let's go, A.J. We'll talk at your place."

CHAPTER SIXTEEN

THEY DIDN'T SPEAK while Mac drove to her building, but he kept her hand in his. She clung to it like a lifeline.

"How about some pizza?" she said as she closed her apartment door behind them.

"Not hungry." He took the box and tossed it on the kitchen table without taking his eyes off her face.

"Something to drink? A beer? A glass of wine?" She was stalling and she knew it.

"Nothing." He got a glass of water and handed it to her. "Let's go sit down, A.J."

His voice had never been so gentle. Avoiding his eyes, she took a drink of water and sat on the couch. The same place, she realized, she'd been sitting the night they'd almost made love there.

Before she could move, he was next to her. Too close. Panic stirred. She wouldn't be able to keep her composure with Mac so close to her.

"How are you doing?" he asked.

Her first impulse was to lie, to smile and tell him she

was fine. To protect herself. But when she looked at him, she didn't see a man guarding his emotions. He was completely open, his fear, his worry and his concern all crossing his face. The least she could do was match his honesty with her own.

"I'm shaking," she said. "I'm angry at myself for getting into that situation. I'm scared, and I'm angry that I've let him scare me."

"I'm scared, too," Mac said, but an undertone of anger was in his voice. "I'm terrified. But you beat him." He smoothed her hair away from her face. "He came after you and you kicked his ass. Remember that."

"He was going to kill me," she said. "I know it." Doak's face swam in front of her, full of hatred and resolve. And an awful glee she'd remember for a very long time. "He wanted to kill me."

"But he didn't. You were smarter and faster than him." His gaze warmed as he watched her. "You're amazing, A.J."

"No, I'm not," she said. She wanted to be completely honest, to hold nothing back. "It wouldn't have happened at all if I hadn't let my temper get the better of me. I should have called you, had you meet me at my yoga class."

"You seem to have a problem with me and your temper," he said. "I hope there's no one else who makes you lose your temper like I do."

"Not a soul," she said, keeping her voice light.

"You're the only one." The only one she'd ever let get under her skin.

"I'm glad."

The emotions she could read in his eyes made her look away. "Thank you for coming so quickly tonight."

"You asked for me when you called 911."

"I thought it was your chance to arrest Doak."

"Is that the only reason you asked for me?"

If she was going to be honest, she might as well go all the way. She closed her eyes, took a deep breath. Then looked directly at him. "No. I needed you, Mac."

"You've got me," he whispered.

He framed her face with his hands. But, instead of pulling her into his arms, he slid his hands down her arms and twined her fingers with his.

"We need to talk about last night," he said.

She tried to pull her hands away, but he wouldn't let go. "It's not going away just because we ignore it," he said.

"It's over."

"Is it?" he asked, brushing his lips over the back of her hand, and making her stomach jump.

"I don't want to do this tonight."

"We have to do this tonight. I don't want it between us." His grip tightened. "If we'd had this conversation last night, you might have waited for me today."

He was right and she knew it. "What happened between us was a mistake. We can agree on that."

"Yes. It was. I wanted to take more care with you when we made love, to give you tenderness and romance. Instead I was blinded by jealousy. And need. I hurt you, and I'll never forgive myself for that. I'm sorry. But it doesn't change the way I feel about you." His thumb rubbed against her knuckles. "Afterward you wouldn't listen to me, and I guess I can't blame you. You pushed me away, and I was stupid enough to go. From now on, I'm not going anywhere."

Tears welled in her eyes and she blinked hard, trying to hold them back. One slipped down her cheek.

"Oh, God, A.J.," he said, finally pulling her into his arms. "It breaks my heart when you cry."

Her face pressed into his shoulder, the scent of him surrounding her, she relaxed and let him fit his body to hers. "I don't cry," she said with a sniffle. "I told you that before." But then, when he bent his head down and kissed her hair, another tear leaked out.

"I wanted to hurt you last night," he murmured. "I wanted you to feel as devastated as I did. I'm so sorry."

"You didn't trust me," she said, leaning back to look at his face. "Why?"

"Because I'm an idiot." He brushed his lips over hers. "A brainless idiot whose only excuse is that he was blinded by lust and maddened by jealousy."

She didn't take her gaze off his face, and he sighed. "I don't trust easily, A.J. I don't get involved. I like to keep things light and simple. I don't take you lightly, and it's never been simple with you. And that scares the hell out of me."

"I'm scared, too, Mac. You matter to me. That's why what happened hurt so much."

"I've never wanted anyone the way I want you. I completely lost control," he whispered. "You make me crazy, sweetheart."

"I'm glad. Because you make me just as crazy."

"I've never been good at letting down my guard," he said. "I've never wanted to. But I'd like to try."

"This is new for me, too. And I'm not sure how to handle it."

He stroked her face. "We'll figure it out together. Can we get past what I did?"

The hard lump of pain lodged inside her loosened. "I think so."

"Forgive me, A.J. Please."

The last of her hurt melted away at the pain in his eyes. "You're forgiven."

"Is it that easy?" he asked, his hands tightening on her.

"Apparently so." She gave him a tremulous smile and brushed a kiss over his lips. Happiness flowed through her like warm honey.

"Can we erase what happened and start over?"

"Maybe we can just go from there." She gave him a slow smile. "There are certain aspects of last night that I don't want to erase."

His eyes fired. "I'd like to hear about them. Later. First, there are a lot of things I've been dreaming about that I didn't do last night."

"What kinds of things?"

Instead of kissing her, as she expected, he pulled her into his lap. "I hate that I didn't look at you. I've fantasized about looking at you for weeks."

"Weeks? Come on, McDougal. Up until a week ago, you could barely stand the sight of me."

"I did a good job, didn't I? You had no idea I was just like the rest of the pitiful slobs in the department who lust after you."

"Is that right?" She shivered as his hand tunneled beneath her T-shirt and settled on one breast. When he brushed a finger over her nipple, she gasped.

"Yeah. You know what else I hate?"

"What?"

"I hate that I didn't touch you. I've ached to touch you." He skimmed a finger over her thigh to the inside of her leg. Heat flared deep inside her, lit by every slow sweep of his finger over her skin.

Need swept through her, consuming every other thought in her head. Finally, when she was trembling beneath his hands, he moved his hand slowly up her body, igniting more fires wherever he lingered. This time, when he reached her chest, he eased his hand beneath her sports bra, closed it around her breast.

"Oh, yeah," he groaned. "I could touch you for hours."

His mouth seduced her, tempted her, lured her. He kissed her as if with his mouth alone he could uncover the essence of who she was.

She melted into him, helpless against such tenderness. He murmured her name as he tasted her neck. Finally, his breath sending shivers across her skin, he picked her up and carried her into the bedroom.

He undressed her slowly, but when the upper half of her body was bared, he leaned back. "And I could spend days just looking at you," he said, his voice husky and uneven.

"I don't want to wait for days." She wanted his mouth on her again. "Are you going to make me beg?"

"Oh, yeah," he whispered as he began to peel the shorts down her legs. "I want to hear you beg."

His mouth trailed over her abdomen, the insides of her legs, the backs of her knees. When she was naked, quivering from his kisses, he knelt between her legs. "I want to taste you, A.J. I want to watch you when you come."

He pressed his mouth to her. She arched off the bed, small cries bursting from her throat.

He stripped off his own clothes, slipping a condom out of his pocket. As he tore it open, she touched him and the hard muscles of his abdomen quivered beneath her fingers. His broad shoulders blocked the light spilling through the door from the other room, but she could see the desire in his eyes. When her hands slid below his waist, he captured them and pinned them above her head.

"It looks like I'm the one who's begging," he said, his voice thick.

She wrapped her legs around him. Joined together, surrounded by each other, filled with each other, they began to move. When she felt herself climaxing, she moaned his name, drew him deeper. Slick with sweat, his muscles tensed beneath her hands, he pressed his mouth to hers, and she exploded with a cry.

MAC HAD NO IDEA how much time had passed. Still inside her, he rolled over so he wouldn't crush her. She sprawled boneless on top of him, her skin hot, her muscles relaxed.

"I don't think I can move," she managed to say. "I'm not sure I'll ever be able to move again."

"At least you can feel your legs," he said as she twined them with his.

He felt her smile against his skin. His heartbeat an unsteady rhythm, and he tightened his hold on her.

"You don't do that often enough."

"Do what?" she asked.

"Smile." He tucked her wild curls behind her ear, let his hand linger on her cheek. "Just smile."

Her mouth curved again. "Looks like you found the switch."

"A.J."

Her face glowing and flushed, she laughed. "Mac."

"I wish I had given you this, given *us* this, last night."

Her smile widened, grew mischievous. "There's nothing wrong with wild monkey sex."

He couldn't believe this was the same controlled woman he saw every day. "We'll test that hypothesis," he said. "As soon as I get the feeling back in my legs."

His hand smoothed over her hair, her neck, trailed down her side and over her hip in a long, lazy sweep. Then he started over again. He felt her breathing even out.

As he stroked her back, he found a hard bump on her skin. Then another and another. He faltered. They weren't bumps. They were more like ridges.

Puzzled, he looked down. Several scars crisscrossed her back.

"A.J.?" he asked, staring at them, his stomach rolling. "What are these scars from? Did someone hurt you?"

She tensed in his arms, then rolled away from him. She sat up and reached for her robe. "That's ancient history," she said, her voice light. "An accident when I was a kid." She licked her lips. "How about some of that pizza?"

Her eyes were too bright and her smile trembled at the corners. There were layers of A.J. to be uncovered, he thought. More than he'd realized. But he was willing to let her reveal them in time.

"Pizza sounds great." He brushed his lips over her hand as he stood up. "We have all night. We can take a break before I make you beg."

CHAPTER SEVENTEEN

THE NEXT MORNING A.J. sat at her desk and smiled as she studied the stack of reports waiting for her. Not even the prospect of a day catching up on paperwork could spoil her mood.

Mac had driven her into work, walked her into the building, then gone home to change his clothes. But the heat from the kiss they'd shared behind the closed door of her office left her longing for more. A knock interrupted her thoughts. "Come in," she called.

Mac opened the door, his face hard. "The Jamisons are here to see you, Ms. Ferguson."

"Send them in," she said, her joy evaporating. Todd's deadline had passed, and she'd asked Mac to arrest him, but Jeanine must have convinced Todd to come in before that could happen.

Todd Ferguson swaggered into her office, a smirk on his face, and threw himself into a chair. No wonder Mac looked pissed, she thought with a sigh. She wasn't surprised at the teen's attitude, but it was guaranteed to push all of Mac's buttons.

His mother followed, her eyes red and swollen from weeping. Mac leaned against the door, scowling.

"Todd, go get a chair for yourself from the other room," A.J. said in a pleasant voice. "Jeanine, Detective McDougal, please take a seat."

Todd's face filled with sullen anger, but when she held his gaze he got up and stalked out the door. Moments later he returned and slammed a chair to the floor.

"Thank you," A.J. said, giving him a nod. "Todd, you were supposed to be here yesterday. Why weren't you?"

He shrugged and slid lower in his chair, his legs sprawled in front of him. "I was busy."

"You were busy. You're not taking this very seriously, Todd." He gave her another smirk. The beginnings of anger stirred and she looked at the papers on her desk. "You're lucky you showed up this morning. Detective McDougal was getting ready to head to your school. To arrest you."

Momentary uncertainty passed over Todd's face, then he shrugged. "Whatever."

Keeping a firm grip on her temper, A.J. turned to Todd's mother. "Jeanine, please summarize Todd's behavior the last several months."

Jeanine nodded and blotted tears out of her eyes. Then she recited a list of infractions that escalated steadily until she reached the day she took his car keys away. Her voice faltered as she touched the fading bruise on her face.

A.J. looked at Todd. "Is this accurate so far?"

"I guess."

A.J. turned back to his mother. "What happened when you took his car keys away?"

Jeanine didn't look at her son. She stared at A.J., her eyes filled with pain and despair. "Todd threw a book at me. At my face."

"Why did you do that, Todd?" A.J. asked.

The boy smirked again. "She's a liar. My mom walked into a door. That's how she got that bruise."

Mac visibly tensed, but A.J. shot him a warning look, and he relaxed.

Pity surged through A.J. Todd was much too young to be spouting the typical words of an abuser. "She told me you hit her, Todd. And I believe her."

"That's your problem," the boy answered.

Anger washed away all the pity. "No, that's your problem." She twined her fingers together on her desk. "Did your mom tell you the deal?"

Contempt flashed in Todd's eyes. "Yeah, she did. I spill my guts to some shrink and you won't slap my wrist."

"And you agree?" A.J. asked.

"Sure. I'll sit in a shrink's office for as long as you want."

"And cooperate?"

"I said I'd be there. That was the deal. I didn't say I'd talk."

"All right, Todd," she said, rubbing the bridge of her nose. "If that's your choice, we'll honor it." She glanced over at Mac. "Go ahead and arrest him, Detective."

Before Mac could stand up, Todd sat up straight in his chair. "He can't arrest me. I didn't do anything."

"You hit your mother, Todd." A.J. held his gaze until he looked away.

Towering over Todd, Mac took out his handcuffs. "Get up, Jamison."

Todd looked at his mother, but she stared at her hands. A flicker of uncertainty appeared in his eyes.

Mac grabbed Todd's collar and yanked him out of the chair. Then he pulled the kid's arms in front of him, clicked the handcuffs into place and pushed him back into the chair. He read him his rights in a monotone.

Jeanine Jamison wept softly.

"This is so bogus," Todd said. "Tell them, Mom."

"Your mother is out of the loop now, kid," Mac said. "After Ms. Ferguson is done, I'm taking you to juvie."

Todd struggled against the handcuffs as fear came into his eyes. "You can't lock me up. My mom isn't going to let you. Right, Mom?"

"There's nothing I can do, Todd." Jeanine pressed a tissue to her eyes. "I tried to tell you this was your last chance. I tried to tell you that you were in trouble. But you didn't care."

"Don't cry to your mommy, you little snot bag,"

Mac said, his voice hard. "She's got nothing to do with this anymore. From now on the judge is your mommy."

"Mom? Are you going to let them do this?" Todd's voice quivered. "Are you going to let them put me in jail?"

"It's not up to me anymore," Jeanine said, her voice muffled by the tissue and her sobs.

"You were given many chances, Todd, and you chose not to take any of them." A.J. was filled with sorrow and anger for the waste of a young life. "Let me tell you about juvie."

She took a deep breath to steady herself as the memories rushed in. "Do you have your own room at home?" she asked.

He nodded.

"At juvie you'll sleep in a dorm, with twenty or thirty other boys. Every time one of them rolls over at night, you'll hear the bed squeak. You'll hear all the new guys crying themselves to sleep." She leaned closer. "You'll *be* one of the new guys crying himself to sleep.

"You'll get up when the guards tell you to get up at 5:30 a.m. You'll eat when they tell you to eat. And, by the way, all the food tastes the same. And none of it tastes like your mom's.

"Your life will be run by the guards. You'll do whatever they tell you to do, when they tell you to do it. And I haven't even started to tell you what the other inmates will be like. How will you deal with guys who would just as soon kill you as look at you?"

She rested back in her chair, satisfied that the insolence had disappeared from Todd's face. Now she saw only fear.

"Mom?" he said in a small voice.

A.J. locked her gaze on Jeanine's, stared her down when she would have turned to Todd.

"I don't want to go there," Todd said, his voice thin with panic. "I want to go home."

Mac spoke from behind him. "You should have thought of that when you were bullying your mom, kid. You should have thought of that when you were giving Ms. Ferguson crap a few minutes ago. You're not so tough now, are you?" He grabbed Todd's arm. "Let's go, punk."

"No!" Todd cried. "Wait!"

"What is it?" A.J. asked.

"I'll talk to someone," he said wildly. "I'll talk to anyone you want me to talk to."

"It's too late to just talk," A.J. said in a calm voice. "You have to want to work on what's wrong. You have to want to fix it."

"I do! I will!" He sniffled once and wiped his nose on the sleeve of his shirt.

A.J. studied him for a moment. Mac still held his arm, tugging on it just enough to let the boy know who was in control. Todd looked like a terrified child. All traces of his insolence had vanished.

"All right," A.J. said. "I'll listen to what you have to say. Detective, Jeanine, why don't you leave us alone for a few minutes?"

As Mac turned to leave the room and his mother rose from her chair, Todd swiveled in his seat and held out his hands to Mac. "Aren't you going to take these off?"

"Hell, no," Mac snapped. "You think I'm leaving you alone with Ms. Ferguson without the cuffs?" He jerked his head toward Jeanine. "I don't want her face looking like your mom's." Mac's eyes were hard and flat and menacing. "I don't like men who hit women, scumbag."

Todd shrank away from him, watching as the door closed behind his mother and Mac. Slowly he turned to face A.J.

"All right, Todd," she said. "Let's talk about why you hit your mother."

A HALF HOUR LATER, the door to A.J.'s office opened. Mac looked up from the report he was finishing and saw her walk over to Jeanine, laying a hand on the woman's shoulder. "Why don't you come into the office?" she said in a soft voice.

Jeanine followed A.J., her steps a little unsteady, and the door closed again.

"Did you put the fear of God into that punk?" Jake asked.

"I hope so." Mac stared at the door. "It would help if his mother found the backbone to do what she has to do."

"Maybe A.J. can help her see that."

Jake sounded as doubtful as Mac felt. Mac sighed as he went back to his report. Optimism was the first casualty of this job. Too many of the stories they heard had unhappy endings.

It was at least another half hour before A.J.'s door opened again. Todd and Jeanine walked out in front of A.J. The kid stared at the ground, his hands still cuffed. His mother held one of his arms, pulling him close to her side.

"You can take the cuffs off now, Detective," A.J. said as they stopped in front of his desk.

Mac stood up, not rushing as he pulled the key out of his pocket. "Are you sure?"

"No," A.J. said. "I'm not."

Todd looked up, panic skittering over his face. But he didn't say anything.

"Todd and his mom have an appointment later this afternoon with a therapist. We're going to give it a try for a week, then reassess. So go ahead and release him."

Mac snapped the cuffs open and shoved them into his pocket. Todd rubbed the red marks on his wrists without looking up.

"Remember what those cuffs felt like, kid," he said.

Mac stood with A.J. as they watched Jeanine and Todd Jamison walk out the door. When they were out of sight, he turned to A.J.

"What do you think? Is he going to end up in juvie?"

"I don't know," she said. "He was cooperative, but once he gets home?" She shrugged. "I hoped this was one case that would have a happy ending. We'll see."

"What happened to your optimism?" Mac asked.

"It disappeared about a hundred abusers ago."

"What's the plan for Todd?" He took her arm and steered her toward her office.

"As I said, he's going to see Jerry Winston. Jerry does a lot of work with teenage boys and I'm hoping he'll be able to help Todd. Jerry will set up a schedule and make sure Todd adheres to it. He'll keep me updated about what's going on."

"And the kid's mom?"

A.J. sighed. "I recommended she see a therapist, too. She took the first step by getting away from Todd's father. But she needs a whole lot more self-esteem in order to deal with Todd effectively." She sank down into her desk chair and rubbed her forehead. "It's getting more and more painful to watch."

Mac closed her office door, then sat down in a chair across from hers. "Why didn't Jeanine Jamison let us throw Todd's worthless butt in juvie for a few days? That would have straightened him out pretty damn quick."

"She loves her son," A.J. said quietly. "She doesn't want to see him locked up."

"Even if it would help solve the problem?"

"Especially then. I'm sure she feels guilty. She probably thinks she contributed to the situation."

"Because she didn't leave his father?" Mac scoffed. "That's no excuse for that junior scumbag."

"I know that, but she's his mother. She loves him. That's the way it's supposed to be for parents, Mac." A.J. looked down at her hands. They were clenched into fists, her knuckles white. Deliberately she relaxed her fingers. "Parents who love their children stand by them, no matter what. They never give up on their kids."

Mac shifted in the chair, stared out the window. "Not where I come from."

"I'm sorry," she said. She stood up and came around the desk. "I know how lonely that is." She touched his face, let her hand linger. "You turned out pretty well in spite of it."

Mac wanted to lean into her touch, to let her warmth fill all the hollow places inside him. But fear held him back, kept him teetering on the edge of an abyss of unfamiliar, frightening emotions.

He stood up. "You did a great job with the kid," he said, combing his hand through his hair. "You scared the hell out of him when you told him about juvie."

"I hoped it would get through to him."

He jittered his foot as he watched her, tension building inside him, fear overwhelming him. "It did. It sounded like you had a real good idea of what went on there. The kind of idea you couldn't get from visiting."

Her face paled before she turned to look out the window. After a long time, she said, "I do."

"How so, A.J.?"

Slowly she faced him. Her dark eyes stood out in stark contrast to her colorless face. "I should have told you a long time ago. I spent time in juvie when I was a teenager."

A cold fist squeezed his heart. "What for?"

"Does it matter?"

She watched him steadily, her eyes unreadable. The abyss he'd balanced on a few moments ago opened into a yawning gulf that spread wider and wider, separating him from her.

He wasn't sure which was worse, the fear that he was losing her or the realization of how much it would hurt if he did. "You tell me if it matters, A.J."

"It looks like it matters to you."

"Hell, yes, it matters to me."

"I understand," she said.

"I don't think you do. What matters to me is that you didn't trust me enough to tell me, without being asked. It's not about what petty crime you committed as a teenager. It's about trust."

"I trust you, Mac," she whispered. She wrapped her arms around herself, as if fending off a chill.

"The hell you do. If you trusted me, you'd let me know the A.J. buried beneath the layers you show everyone else." He took a deep breath, welcoming the anger, allowing it to hold off the pain for a while longer. "Hell, I don't know why I'm surprised. You won't even tell me your name."

He grabbed the knob and yanked the door open. "I'll be out here when you're ready to go home."

He pulled the door closed behind him and slumped into his desk chair. Jake took one look at him and shook his head. "The course of true love, blah, blah, blah."

"Don't you say another word."

"There's nothing else to say."

"With you there's always something else to say. And right now I don't want to hear it."

Mac stared at the stack of files on his desk, not seeing any of them. He could run a check on A.J. He could look up her juvenile records, find out why she was in juvie.

His stomach twisted at the thought of betraying her like that. No matter what she'd done, he couldn't do that.

The phone on his desk rang, and he grabbed it out of its cradle, grateful for the diversion. "McDougal."

"Mac, I have some preliminary reports on the homicide victim from yesterday," the medical examiner said. "Want me to go over them?"

"Thanks, Beth," he said, closing his eyes. He was a coward, but he leaped at the excuse to put off his confrontation with A.J. "Jake and I will come see you."

He hung up. "Let's go, Jake. Beth has something for us."

Jake nodded toward the closed door of A.J.'s office. "You're not going to see her home?"

A tiny voice called him a coward, but he blocked it out. "I'll have one of the patrol guys take her home and check her apartment."

"Yeah?"

Mac saw the pity in his partner's eyes and scowled. "We have a case to close," he snarled at Jake. "My personal life isn't going to get in the way."

Jake studied him. "You'd better get your priorities straight, son. Or your personal life won't be there when we close this case."

Ignoring him, Mac knocked on A.J.'s door but didn't wait for an answer before he opened it and stuck his head in. "I have to leave. One of the patrol guys will drive you home, then stay to keep an eye on your building."

"All right."

Her voice was muted, and she didn't meet his gaze. She swiveled her chair so she faced the window, but he caught a glimpse of her eyes. They were red and swollen.

As if she'd been crying.

"A.J.," he began, but she interrupted him.

"You need to go, Mac." She gripped the arms of the chair. "You have work to do."

Don't go, the tiny voice ordered. *Stay with her.*

Instead he backed out the door and closed it behind him.

CHAPTER EIGHTEEN

DOAK DROVE PAST the police station, slowing as he scanned the cars in the lot. There it was. The little blue sports car parked under the streetlight assured him that the Ferguson woman wouldn't be in his way.

He drove straight to her apartment. The parking lot was almost empty. There were only a few scattered cars—and none of them were squad cars.

It was easy enough to get past the security door and into the building. He simply rang all the bells and waited for someone to push the buzzer. He smiled as he got into the elevator. There was always someone gullible enough to open the door.

He stopped outside her door and knocked lightly, even though he'd seen her car at the station. He wouldn't take any stupid chances. He was too smart for that.

When nothing stirred in the apartment and no one answered the door, he knocked again. Then, glancing up and down the hall, he used the tool he'd bought from a locksmith and opened the door.

He stood inside the apartment, savoring his power. He could get into her space any time he chose.

Which meant she was completely at his mercy. Excitement swelled inside him, tangling with anger. The next time he saw the Ferguson bitch, she wouldn't toss him on his back and kick him in the head.

The next time he saw her, it would be on his terms.

Once he dealt with Mindy and Jamie, he'd come back for her.

But first he had to find Mindy and the kid.

If the woman in the tatty robe at the shelter *had* been Mindy, she didn't have Jamie with her. It was possible he'd missed the kid in the confusion of the fire. It was also possible that they were keeping him somewhere else.

If the kid told the cops what he'd seen, they'd be keeping a close eye on him.

Rage stirred inside him. They wouldn't keep him away from his kid.

He walked through the apartment until he came to a tiny bedroom that held a desk and some bookcases.

He sat down at the desk and went through every drawer, every pile of papers. The Ferguson woman was organized, he'd say that for her. But there was nothing that even hinted at the location of Mindy and Jamie.

Frustrated and angry, he started to sweep the papers off the top of the desk, but he stopped himself in time. He couldn't afford to indulge his anger.

He left the papers in tidy piles, then walked into the kitchen. Next to the telephone was a caller ID unit, and he picked it up and scrolled through her calls.

The only name he recognized was the Tarrington Hotel. Instead of clicking past it, he stared at it, wondering. Would they have put Mindy and Jamie into a hotel after the fire at the shelter?

It was possible, he thought with growing excitement. It was possible.

He scribbled down the other names and phone numbers, just in case, then slipped out of the apartment. He'd pay a visit to the Tarrington. If he were lucky, his family would be waiting there for him.

"ALL CLEAR, MA'AM."

A.J. tossed her briefcase on the couch. "Thank you, Terry," she said to the earnest young police officer who'd seen her home. "I appreciate this."

"No problem. I'll be outside if you need me."

"Thanks," she said again as the officer closed the door behind him.

Silence echoed in her apartment, a silence that cut bone deep. She reached for the television, turning it on, needing the sound of voices. But her steps faltered when she entered her bedroom.

Mac haunted the room. Their mingled scent lingered in the air, and her throat swelled as she hurried to change her clothes. In the kitchen, memories of him comforting her swamped her. Trying to banish them, she nuked some leftovers but only managed to eat a couple of bites.

Afterward she prowled her apartment, unable to settle down. She wasn't interested in any of the television shows. She couldn't concentrate on the book she'd been reading. There were no chores waiting to be done.

The only thing she could think about was Mac. How he'd tasted, how he'd felt when he held her close. How he looked when he asked her why she'd been in juvie. The pain in his eyes when she hadn't answered his question.

He'd been angry. But beneath the anger had been hurt and disappointment.

He was right. She hadn't trusted him to react like her lover instead of a cop.

She'd been holding herself back, protecting herself. She hadn't wanted to give Mac that much control over her. He already held a frightening amount of power. It would take only a few words from him to destroy her.

She'd never been a coward.

She wasn't going to start with Mac.

She couldn't wait another moment. She had to see him. She wanted to tell him everything about herself, reveal the secrets that only a few people knew.

It was time to take a chance, time to step out on the ledge.

Time to jump, and trust Mac to catch her.

SHE PULLED INTO THE DRIVEWAY of a small bungalow in one of Riverton's older neighborhoods, studying the house. Mac's home was well cared for. The bushes were neatly trimmed, the flowers in front of them were bright and cheery, and the wooden trim around the windows and doors was freshly painted.

She'd bet he did all the work himself.

Mac's truck loomed in front of her on the driveway, dwarfing her sports car. So he was home. She didn't have an excuse for backing up and driving away.

Drawing in a shaky breath, she got out of the car and closed the door carefully. Her hand trembled as she dropped her keys into her purse, and the patrol car idled at the curb, waiting.

She rang the bell and heard footsteps approaching the door. Mac opened it.

"May I come in?" she asked.

He didn't move for a heartbeat. Then he swung the door wide. A.J. waved to the police officer at the curb before she squeezed past Mac's arm and stepped into the house.

The floors were hardwood, the glowing tones catching and reflecting the late afternoon sun back at her. There was a couch and chair in the living room, and an old table with four chairs stood in the middle of the dining room. Small area rugs covered the floor in both rooms. There were pictures on the walls and a television and bookcases in the living room.

It was spare and nothing fancy, but Mac had made it into a home.

"What are you doing here, A.J.?" Mac asked. His voice was even and she couldn't hear any emotion in it.

She stared out the window, her hands clenched into fists inside her pockets. "When I was put in juvie, my name was Angelina Janelle. Angelina Janelle Moody. I changed it legally to A.J. after I got out of juvie. Angelina Janelle was gone. I wasn't that person anymore and I didn't want to remember when I was."

She took a deep, shuddering breath. "I was sent to juvie because—"

"Stop, A.J. You don't have to do this. I'm not going to force you to tell me about your past." He turned her to face him and kept his hands on her shoulders. "I was way out of line earlier when I got angry at you. I haven't told you everything about me, either. What happened before we met doesn't matter."

"You're wrong, Mac," she said quietly. "It does matter. It matters for a lot of reasons."

She wanted, so badly, to let Mac wrap his arms around her, let him comfort her.

He deserved more than that, so she stepped away.

"I want you to know me. And you can't know me unless you know who I used to be. I should have told you a long time ago." She swallowed. "I should have told you last night when you noticed the scars on my back. I wish I had.

"I didn't tell you at first because I know how you feel about criminals. I didn't want to be someone on the other side of the line, one of *them*. I didn't want you to look at me with those cop's eyes of yours."

"You're not a criminal, sweetheart."

She swallowed and continued before she lost her nerve. "Then I told myself I couldn't tell you because of the rules. The ones that say police officers can't hang around with felons. Since I wanted to be with you, I figured it would be better if you didn't know I was a felon."

She sighed, gave him a painful smile. "I was making excuses. The real reason I didn't tell you was that I was afraid. You were becoming too important to me, and I didn't want to do anything to change your opinion of me."

"I never knew you were a drama queen, A.J." He reached out, skimmed a finger down her cheek. "Maybe you were arrested when you were a kid, but you can't be a felon. You work for the police department."

"The people who hired me know about my past. Juvenile records are sealed, but I wanted them to know. They said it didn't matter, as long as I wasn't a sworn member of the department." She tried to smile and failed miserably. "That doesn't mean I can fraternize with the police officers. You were off-limits."

"That's my A.J.," he murmured, sliding his arms around her. "I love it when you break the rules."

The warmth in his eyes made her cringe with guilt. "This isn't a joke, Mac." She wished to God it was.

He steered her to the couch and eased her down. "Okay, you're a felon. What was this crime you didn't want to tell me about?" His mouth curled into a faint smile. "Did you shoplift some clothes from one of the department stores? Did you vandalize your high school? Go joyriding in a car that didn't belong to you? Get caught at a party with drugs?"

She kept her gaze on his. "I killed my father."

The understanding faded from his eyes, replaced by shock. *"What?"*

"I stabbed my father to death. They said it was pre-meditated because I had a knife under my bed. I was fourteen years old, and I was in juvie for four years."

"My God, A.J." His arm tightened around her as he stared at her with horror and pity.

She looked away, unable to bear what she saw. She'd known he'd look at her like that, like she was a freak. "He was a classic abuser. I don't remember a time when he wasn't hitting my mother, or me. Then I got older, and it changed." Nausea rolled over her at the long-suppressed memory.

"Did he rape you?"

"No. He never raped me." She met his gaze squarely. "But he was working up to it. That's why I kept the knife under my bed. I was only fourteen, but I knew. He came into my room one night when my mother was at work. I woke up and saw it in his eyes." Remembered horror swept over her. "So I stabbed him."

"They sent you to juvie because you protected yourself?"

The pity in his eyes made her skin crawl with shame. "It was fifteen years ago, Mac. People thought of domestic violence in a different way. My public defender was fresh out of law school and overwhelmed. He recommended I accept the plea bargain."

"And your mother let this happen? She let them arrest you and lock you up for four years? Why didn't she tell anyone what had been going on?"

"My mother needed to protect herself. She needed to ignore what was happening." A.J. swallowed. The memory of that betrayal still filled her with pain.

"So your mother let them send you to juvie for killing your abuser." His voice was flat and cold.

"I think she was glad he was dead and drowning in guilt because she'd let him beat me. It was easier not to deal with it, to forget it—*me*—and move on." It was the thin comfort she'd clung to during the lonely nights in juvie, listening to the other girls cry, trying not to cry herself.

"Your mother didn't stand up for you, did she?" He brushed her hair away from her face. "Is that why you stand up for abused women and children?"

She looked down at her hands, remembered how they'd looked covered with her father's blood. "I guess it is."

"What happened to your mother?"

"I know what you're thinking. You want to see her punished." She sucked in a shaky breath. "It's too late for that. She hooked up with another abuser after I was locked up. He killed her two years later."

Mac stood and shoved his hands into his pockets. The sun was beginning to set and golden rays touched his face. "You must have thought I was a real jerk, complaining about my miserable childhood when yours was so much worse."

"No. Just because your pain was different than mine doesn't make it less real. I meant every word I said."

"A.J.—" he began, but she stopped him.

"I need to finish this," she said. "I was a handful at juvie. I got into a lot of trouble at first. I was so relieved that my father was dead, that he wouldn't hurt me anymore. And so guilty because I was happy about it. Because I was the one who killed him. There was a woman at juvie, a social worker. They made me go see her, and at first I was just like Todd Jamison—surly, insolent. A real smart-ass. But she kept trying until I broke down one day in front of her. For the first time, I talked to her. It started to get better after that."

"Is she the one who got you started with martial arts?"

A.J. nodded. "She thought it would be good for me. For my self-esteem, for my confidence." She gave him a wry smile. "So I could protect myself without a knife."

She took a deep breath. "That's who I was with the other night at the restaurant. Her name's Kate Ferguson."

"She was related to you?" Mac asked with a puzzled look.

A genuine smile curved her mouth. "She is now. Kate adopted me after my mother was killed." She cleared her throat. "The man who took me home that night is her fiancé."

He looked away from her. "I really screwed up, didn't I?"

"It doesn't matter," she said. Although it did. Deep down, it still hurt that he hadn't trusted her. And now she'd hurt him with a similar lack of trust.

"Yeah, it matters, A.J." He paced to the window.

"Those scars on your back." He spoke without looking at her. "Your father did that to you?"

"Yes."

"Why didn't you tell me, A.J.? Why didn't you let me share your pain? Did you think I couldn't handle the truth?"

Her throat tightened and swelled. "I'm like you. I don't trust easily, Mac. Especially when it's important. And you're more important than…" *Than anything.* But she couldn't say the words, not yet, not with him so far away. She could touch him, but he would still be miles away from her.

"Don't you know me at all?" he said, his voice raw.

"Did you think I would look at you and see a murderer, not an abused child? Did you think I wouldn't see the woman you are today? Do you think I'm that shallow?"

He stared at her, his eyes full of pain. "Or is it that you think I'm not strong enough to accept the fact that you're not perfect? Do you think my feelings for you are so superficial that I'll run at the first sign of trouble?"

He shoved his hand through his hair and turned away. "Are you too proud to lean on me, to let me share your burdens? Or am I not enough for you?"

"You're the strongest man I know," she whispered. "You're everything…." *Everything I want and need.*

She couldn't force the words out of her mouth. Years of caution, years of protecting herself, her heart, stole her voice.

"Hell, A.J." He scrubbed his hands over his face. "I told you I don't do relationships," he said wearily. "I should have known better than to try." The hurt beneath his words filled the room, clutched at her heart.

"No," she said. "This is my fault. I was wrong." She went to the window and took his hand. "I let my fear get in the way of what I felt. I diminished you because I was afraid."

He turned his palm to hers, laced their fingers together. "Where do we go from here, A.J.?"

"I don't know. I've never been in this place before. No one's ever mattered this much."

She felt naked in front of him, completely vulnerable. "I don't want to throw this away," she said. "Do you?"

"No," he said, his voice barely audible. "I don't."

"Can you forgive me?"

His hesitation belied his answer. "Yeah, I can forgive you."

"You don't sound sure."

"I'm not sure about anything right now."

Her head ached, along with her heart. She couldn't face the uncertainty in his eyes. Fear and pride kept her silent, and she retreated behind a familiar wall. "You need to concentrate on Doak. Our personal lives have to wait."

Tell me I'm more important than Doak, she pleaded silently. *Tell me this matters more.*

"Yeah," he said, and he couldn't quite disguise the relief. "Let's get this whole Doak thing settled. Then we can figure out where to go."

"Fine." She felt uncertain. She didn't want to leave. Didn't want to walk out that door. Tentatively she reached for him, but her hand only brushed his shoulder as he moved away.

"I'll follow you home," he said.

Her eyes swimming, she headed blindly for the door. *Please, hold me. Ask me to stay,* she begged silently.

She fumbled with the doorknob, praying Mac would stop her. But she stepped outside and walked to her car

without speaking. If she said anything, she would beg.
And she didn't have the courage to do that.

As she drove home, she watched Mac's truck in her
rearview mirror. He stayed close behind her, but the distance between them grew wider and wider. And when
she opened the door to her apartment and he walked
away, the distance between them seemed to stretch for-
ever.

CHAPTER NINETEEN

MAC LEANED BACK in his desk chair the next day, frustrated by the stack of reports piled in front of him. He wasn't in the mood for paperwork. He couldn't concentrate on any of it.

He gaze slid again to the door of A.J.'s office. She'd come in, murmured a greeting to him, then disappeared behind that closed door. She hadn't come out since.

He wanted desperately to see her. But he didn't have the nerve to knock on her door.

He'd screwed up yesterday. Badly screwed up. Again. She'd hurt him and his first impulse had been to protect himself. He should have told her the past didn't matter. He should have held her while she told her story. Instead, he'd closed himself off, aching from his own pain.

He'd never realized he was a coward, and the knowledge devastated him. He shouldn't have let her walk out his door last night. He should have taken her in his arms, told her they'd work it out somehow. He should have told her she was more important than Doak.

He'd been afraid. Afraid of being rejected. Afraid of being hurt.

Afraid to take a chance.

Maybe his instincts had been right all along—keep it casual, keep it light, don't get involved. He wasn't a relationship kind of guy. And this was the proof.

If ever there was a woman meant for him, it was A.J. They fit together perfectly. He found her endlessly fascinating, he connected with her on every level.

And sex was only part of it, even though the heat they generated made him dizzy just thinking about it. Instead of merely satisfying his curiosity, making love with her had only intensified his need for her.

She wasn't afraid of his temper or afraid to go toe-to-toe with him. And she'd stood up for him to his parents, refusing to be intimidated by them.

She was the best thing that had ever happened to him. And he'd ruined his chance with her.

Brooding, he shuffled through the folders, looking for something to distract him. The sound of someone clearing his throat made him look up.

"Pierce."

His father stood in front of his desk, looking uncharacteristically unsure of himself.

"Dad." Mac studied him, wondering why he looked so nervous.

"I need to talk to you," his father said abruptly.

"Is something wrong?"

"You could say that." He glanced at the other detectives and the patrol officers in the bull pen. "But I don't want to discuss it in public."

"There's an interrogation room we can use," Mac said, standing.

His father raised his eyebrows. "Will you enjoy that, Pierce? Putting me into an interrogation room?"

Mac had spent all his emotion worrying about A.J. He had none left to spare on his father's sarcasm. "It's the only private place around here," he said wearily. "The only place we won't be overheard or interrupted."

"Fine," his father said, a shadow of embarrassment flickering across his face.

Mac led the way to the last room on the corridor, turned on the lights and let his father enter in front of him. He closed the door firmly behind himself.

"What it is?" he asked. "Is Mom all right?"

"Your mother is fine." His father studied him for a moment. "Is something wrong, Pierce? You look drained."

"I've been spending a lot of time on Doak." He shifted in his chair and moved a pencil around on the table.

"That's why I'm here," his father said. "I have some information for you. I believe Doak might be staying at one of these motels." He listed several names and addresses without meeting Mac's eyes. "He's used them all before." He cleared his throat. "And he's driving an old, broken-down car. It's brown. I didn't get the complete license plate, but the first three letters are *SJB*."

"Why are you telling me this now?" Mac asked, leaning back in the chair and studying his father. "You made it clear that your loyalties were with Doak."

"I didn't believe he'd hurt Mindy or his boy until I heard what happened to your friend A.J. the other night," he said. "How Doak attacked her."

"Where did you hear that?"

"Let's just say I have my sources. And I prefer not to disclose them."

"So what happened to A.J. made you come in and give me this information?" He glanced down at the notes he'd taken. "You know that with this, we'll probably be able to find Doak."

"I hope so. I don't want him to hurt your friend again."

Mac slowly raised his eyes. "Why?"

His father couldn't mask his impatience. "Because you care about her. That was obvious the night you came to dinner. And she cares about you. That was equally obvious." He cleared his throat. "She stood up for you and told me I was wrong. Not many people say that to me."

Something softened inside Mac as he studied his father. "I never hesitated to tell you."

To his shock, a tiny smile hovered around the corners of his father's mouth. "Believe me, son, I'm aware of that."

"So you're willing to give up your partner, take a financial hit, because you don't want Doak to hurt A.J.?"

A pained expression replaced the smile on his father's face. "Is that so hard to understand? I have other projects in hand. You're my only son. You care about this young woman. I don't want anything to happen to her."

"Thank you, Dad," Mac said, stumbling over the last word.

"You're welcome, Pierce." He stood up. "I have a meeting to attend. After you apprehend Doak, bring A.J. over for dinner again."

Mac's heart squeezed in his chest "I doubt I'll be seeing A.J. when this is over."

His father tilted his head. "What happened?" he asked. His voice was almost gentle.

Mac shoved his hands into his pockets and stood up. "I screwed up."

His father gave him a weary smile. "We all screw up, son. If you love her, you'll work it out."

"I hope so." Mac took a deep breath. "I'll call Mom. If A.J. isn't in the picture, I'll come alone."

"Your mother would like that very much. It would mean a lot to her if you called." The older man hesitated at the door. "I want you to be happy," he finally said.

He walked out before Mac could answer. Mac sank back in his chair. He hadn't realized his father could read him so easily.

The past couple of days had been full of revelations.

AN HOUR LATER he'd just put the phone down after talking to the Department of Motor Vehicles about Doak's car when A.J. stepped out of her office. The green suit she wore made her dark hair gleam, and her shoes made her legs look like they went all the way up to her armpits. Cursing himself, he looked away.

"I just talked to Cissy Gregory," she said, her voice even. "She agreed to let you talk to Jamie."

"Great." Thank God, an excuse to get away. He shoved back from his desk and started toward the door.

"She said I had to be there, too," A.J. called after him.

He stopped and turned slowly. "Why is that?"

"I'm not sure," she answered. "But she didn't sound good. Maybe she needs someone to talk to."

"She can talk to me."

She studied him coolly, as if assessing his ability to comfort Cissy. "You'll be busy with Jamie."

Mac scowled. "Fine. Let's go."

A.J. grabbed her briefcase, then followed him down the stairs. They drove the short distance to the hotel in silence. She stared straight ahead, her hands gripping her briefcase. He couldn't read her expression.

She kept a careful distance away from him as they walked down the hotel corridor. And when he knocked on Cissy's door, she hung back a few steps.

He swiveled to face her. "What's this 'keep away from me' stuff? Afraid I'll bite?" he snarled at her, regret and fear clawing at his belly. "Don't worry. I don't do that in public. I save it for more private moments."

Before she could answer, the door opened and Cissy stood back to let them enter. She looked like hell. Her face was thinner, drawn and pale, and dark shadows ringed her eyes. "Thank you for coming," she said quietly.

Jamie sat on the floor cross-legged, watching television. When he saw Mac and A.J., his face brightened.

"Can we play Transformers again?"

"Sure." Mac lowered himself to the floor, and the boy switched off the television before dragging a box of jumbled plastic pieces from beneath the table.

"How are you doing, Jamie?" Mac asked as he snapped together something that looked like a cross between a dinosaur and a tank.

"Fine." Jamie watched Mac assemble the toy and then reached out and picked it up. He ran his finger down the spines on its back, letting his fingers bump over each one.

Mac waited, excluding everything but Jamie from his consciousness. A.J. and Cissy's murmured voiced faded away, the hotel room faded away, leaving only the pale, tense child in front of him. "That guy needs a buddy," Mac said, nodding at the toy. "Do you have another one of those things to put together?"

Jamie laid several mismatched pieces on the floor

and Mac snapped them together. "There you go. They can help each other fight off the bad guys."

Jamie nodded solemnly. "There are lots of bad guys."

Mac remembered what A.J. had said about Jamie's nightmares and knew the boy wasn't talking about his toys.

"Everybody needs help with the bad guys," he murmured. He lined the two toys up so they stood shoulder to shoulder. "There you go. They'll help each other."

Jamie looked up at him. "Do you ever need help?" he asked.

"All the time."

"You told me when you were here before that I could help you." He watched Mac with huge, wary eyes.

"I'd love to have you help me. I need lots of help."

"I saw him when he buried the treasure," Jamie whispered.

"Who did you see, Jamie?"

Jamie swallowed. "My dad."

"How do you know he was burying treasure?"

"I heard him tell my mom. He was yelling at her. He said she'd taken his treasure. He was going to hit her, so I yelled at him. I told him that my mom didn't take his treasure because I saw him bury it."

"What did your dad do then?" Mac asked, holding his breath.

"He told me that the treasure was a secret. He told

me that he'd hit me if I told anyone about it." A tear slid down his cheek. "I didn't tell you before because I didn't want him to hit me."

"He's not going to hurt you ever again, Jamie. You or your mom. I promise you." Mac gently touched the boy's shoulder, squeezed it. "Okay?"

Jamie sniffled and nodded. Mac picked up the two toys and pretended they were fighting off a common enemy. "So where did your dad bury his treasure?" he asked casually.

Jamie took one of the toys and began moving it. "In our backyard. By my swing set."

"That wasn't very smart of him, was it?" Mac said.

"Why not?" Jamie asked.

"He should have known that a smart kid like you would find it when you played on your swing set."

"I would have found it," Jamie said, nodding his head. "I would have. But then we left."

"But I bet you know right where to look for it when you go home."

Jamie nodded vigorously. "There's dirt underneath the swing. That's 'cause I drag my feet," he confided. "I'm not supposed to drag my feet, but sometimes I go too fast. He buried the treasure under the dirt." He crashed one of the toys into the other. "That's why I would have found it right away," he added, his voice filled with scorn.

Mac sat on the floor with Jamie for a while longer,

putting the Transformers together, playing with him. When all trace of shadows had left the boy's eyes, he touched the boy's shoulder again. "I have to go now," he said. "I'll come back and play with you again. If that's all right with you."

Jamie nodded eagerly. "Tomorrow?"

"Maybe not tomorrow. But real soon. Okay?"

"Okay." He watched as Mac stood up, then went back to his game.

Mac walked over to where A.J. and Cissy sat at the table. "We have to go," he said.

A.J. looked up at him quickly, searching his face. Then she nodded and turned back to Cissy. "I'll call you and set up a time to get together with you in the next day or two," she said. "Is that all right?"

"Thank you," Cissy murmured. She looked slightly less stressed than when they'd walked into the room.

Cissy looked at Mac. "How much longer before you catch Doak?"

"Soon, I hope. I got some information this morning that will narrow the search. And Jamie was very helpful."

"All right. Thank you." She suddenly looked much older. "We can't take much more of this waiting."

"I know. We'll do our best."

As soon as they were out the door, he grabbed A.J.'s elbow and hurried down the hall. She slipped away from him. "What's going on?"

"I need to call Jake."

They were barely out the hotel door before he flipped open his phone and pushed a number. When Jake answered, he said, "Get a search warrant, then get some people out to Talbott's house. They need to start digging under the swing set. Wherever the grass is worn away. I'll be there as soon as I can."

"What did Jamie tell you?" A.J. asked as she climbed into the truck.

"He saw Doak bury something beneath the swing set." He pressed his lips together. "And he didn't like the fact that Jamie saw him. He threatened him."

He flipped on the siren and the lights in the back window as he pressed the accelerator to the floor. As they raced through Riverton, he repeated his conversation with Jamie. When they reached the Talbotts' house, he jumped out. "Stay here," he barked to A.J. without looking at her. Then he ran into the backyard.

Jake stood by a hole in the ground, holding a black plastic trash bag. His face was grim as he looked inside it. "I don't know what Doak was really saying to Mindy, but the kid was right about one thing. This is Doak's treasure, all right," he said.

"What is it?" Mac asked.

"Clothes. Clothes that are badly stained. If I'm not mistaken, and I don't think I am, clothes that are covered in blood."

Mac reached into his back pocket and pulled out a pair of latex gloves. Then he reached into the bag and pulled out a man's shirt. It was stiff and covered with large brown stains.

Mac stared at it for a moment, then let it drop back into the bag. "Bingo," he said softly. "If this blood matches Helena Tripp's, we've got him."

"Yeah," Jake said. He stared at the large, imposing house. "Now all we have to do is find him."

Mac heard A.J. walk up behind him and instinctively moved closer to her. "He knows we're closing in," he said softly. "And now we know why he was so desperate to find Jamie. That's why he went after A.J."

Without looking at A.J., he reached for her. His fingers closed around her wrist, tightened. "He thinks A.J. will lead him to Jamie. That means A.J. isn't out of our sight until Doak is behind bars."

"Right." Jake took out a piece of evidence tape, scribbled the date, time and place on it, then signed it and handed it to Mac, who signed it as well. Then he carefully wrapped it around the bag.

"I'll take this in to the lab and get them started on it," Jake said.

"I got more information this morning," Mac said. "Places Doak might be staying. And a description and partial license plate for the car he's using. I called DMV. They're generating a list of cars that match."

Jake raised his eyebrows as Mac passed on the information. "You've been a busy boy."

"Yeah. Let's get working on this stuff."

He gave instructions to the patrol officers to begin searching the grounds of the Talbott home for any further evidence. Then he turned to A.J., still holding her wrist.

"I'll take you back to the office if you promise to stay there. I don't want you to leave unless I'm with you. Or Jake."

"I won't leave," she said quietly.

He didn't let go of her as they walked back to the car. He slid his palm against hers, was encouraged when she twined her fingers with his.

"Are Jamie and Cissy going to be safe?" she asked as she let go of his hand and slid into the car.

"I hope so. No one else knows where they are."

"Doak seems to be able to find out a lot of things he's not supposed to know."

"This time we're a step ahead of him."

He felt her swivel in her seat to face him, but he didn't look at her.

"Where did you get that information about the car and the motels?" she asked.

He hesitated for a moment too long. "My father came in this morning."

"I see," she said. She turned to stare out the window.

"No, you don't see," he said sharply. "I wasn't trying to keep it from you. I just didn't have a chance to tell you."

The car echoed with her silence. "All right, I could

have told you on the way to see Jamie. I should have told you," he sighed. "I'm not used to talking about stuff with anyone besides Jake."

"You don't have to explain, Mac."

"Yeah, I do. You're involved in this case. You had a right to know."

"I'm not involved in the investigation or the police work," she said, her voice expressionless. "There was no reason to tell me."

"You're wrong," he said, his voice quiet. Desperation clawed at him as he glanced at her. "You're involved at every level. I thought we were a team."

"Did you?"

They'd reached the parking lot at the station, and A.J. jumped out before he could say anything more. She walked into the building without looking back.

He wanted to run after her, to make her look at him again. He wanted to erase the distance between them, knock down the wall that he'd erected to keep her out. He wanted to touch her again, to feel her come alive in his arms.

Instead he drove away. His personal life couldn't take priority right now. He had a job to do.

And chasing Doak Talbott was a lot less scary than offering his heart and soul to A.J. Ferguson.

CHAPTER TWENTY

A.J. OPENED THE DOOR to her apartment and walked inside, Jake right behind her. She tossed her briefcase on the couch and gave him a tired smile.

"I suppose you want to make sure Doak isn't hiding beneath the bed?"

He didn't smile back. "Damn right I do. Mac would skin me alive if I didn't."

"Mac takes his job very seriously." She tried and failed to disguise the pain in her voice.

"Hold on a minute, A.J."

"What?"

"Cut the guy a little slack," he said quietly. "I don't know what happened between the two of you, but it's tearing him apart. And you don't look so hot yourself."

"Leave it alone, Jake," she said wearily.

"No can do." He studied her for a long moment. "I care about him. And about you, too."

She wanted to tell Jake to leave. She didn't want sympathy and understanding. She wanted to be left alone with her pain. Instead she sank down on the couch.

"It's not going to work, Jake. I told him things about me. Things I'm not proud of. Things that happened to me when I was a kid." She hesitated, groping for the right words.

"You don't have to tell me anything," he said, sitting down next to her. "I know you had a rough past."

She looked down at her skirt, rubbing at a smudge of dirt. "It's not that I don't trust you, Jake. I do. But it's still a little raw."

"I don't want to get between you and Mac. Unless you want me to beat him up for you?" Jake raised one eyebrow.

She couldn't resist smiling at her silliness. "I doubt it would do any good. He's a little hard-headed."

Jake snorted. "That's like saying Chicago is a little windy. Don't give up on him. He needs you in his life."

She blinked furiously. "I'm not sure Mac needs anyone in his life."

"You might be surprised." He squeezed her shoulder, then stood up. "Give him a chance, A.J. He's a slow learner, but he does eventually catch on."

She gave him a shaky smile. "Thanks, Jake. I'll keep that in mind."

"Let me go through your apartment, then I'll leave you alone and vegetate on your couch with the television remote. I need to let my mind rot." He gave her a grin. "Promise you're not going to sit here and brood?"

"No brooding." She stood up. "I gave up brooding a long time ago."

"There's another reason Mac needs you. You need to whip him into shape. He's got brooding down to a science."

Moments later Jake emerged from the back hall. "All's clear."

"Thanks, Jake." She brushed her lips across his cheek. "You're a good friend. To both Mac and me."

"Hey, I'm just looking for a safer work environment. If you and Mac don't get straightened out, he's going to take a swing at me before long."

She picked up her briefcase. It was full of files. She'd gotten very little work done today. "I have some paperwork to do," she said, rubbing her temple. "I'll be in the back bedroom."

After changing into a pair of baggy shorts and a loose T-shirt, she went into the small bedroom that served as her office and dropped her briefcase on the floor. As soon as she sat down at the desk, dread filled her.

"Jake?" she called.

"Yo."

"Could you come back here for a minute?"

"What's up?" he asked as he appeared in the doorway.

"I think someone has been in my apartment."

The laid-back man morphed instantly into the detective. "Why do you think so?"

She gestured at the papers on her desk. "These aren't

arranged the way I left them. I have a system. I had them separated into piles—bills that needed to be paid, letters that had to be answered, things to mark on my calendar. And everything's been moved around. It's not obvious if you just glance at the desk, which is why you didn't notice. But I can tell someone has been here."

He pulled out his cell phone and punched in a number. After a moment he said curtly, "Mac. We're at A.J.'s apartment. Get over here right now." He closed the phone without waiting for an answer.

"Go through everything on the desk. Make sure nothing's missing."

MAC CERTAINLY WASN'T in any hurry, she thought with resentment. And sorrow. She had time to go through not only her desk but the rest of her apartment. As far as she could tell, nothing was missing. She sat on the couch, answering Jake's questions, jiggling her leg as she tried not to look at the clock. But as the minutes stretched out into an hour, her heart slowly shriveled inside her chest.

"Something must have happened," Jake said, glancing at her with a worried look. "Or he would be here by now."

"I know he's busy," she murmured, her nails digging into her palm. "I know he can't just drop everything."

"You don't know squat." Jake paced around the small living room. "He knows it has something to do with you. Where the hell is he?"

Just then they heard the ping of the elevator, followed by footsteps pounding down the hall. "A.J.? Jake? Let me in."

Jake threw open the door and Mac rushed in, his gaze zeroing in on her. In moments he was crouched next to her.

"What is it?" he asked A.J. He touched her face, her shoulder, her hand. "Are you hurt? What happened?"

"I'm fine," she said, her voice suddenly shaky. "Jake's fine." She couldn't tear her gaze away from Mac's face, from the sick worry in his eyes. A bit of the weight on her chest lifted. "Someone has been in my apartment."

His hand tightened on hers almost painfully. Then he stood up without letting her go. "Show me."

She led the way to the back bedroom. She pointed at the piles of papers on the desk. "Everything's out of order. Someone looked through my papers and rearranged them."

"What about the rest of the apartment. Anything missing? Anything else out of place?"

"A few things are out of place, but nothing's missing," Jake interjected, his voice as cold as she'd ever heard it. "Which you would know already if you hadn't taken your sweet time getting here."

"Can it, Jake," Mac said, his voice distracted as he turned to look around the room. "I knew you were with her, and I was talking to a witness out at the country club. As much as I wanted to drop everything and run, I couldn't just blow him off."

Mac moved into the bedroom, towing her along behind him. She didn't want to be in this room with Mac. The memories crowding into her head were too bittersweet. But Mac didn't notice. When she tried to tug her hand away from his, he just tightened his grip.

They walked through the kitchen, as well, then all three of them sat down in the living room. Mac pulled her close to him and wrapped one arm around her shoulders almost absently.

"We have to assume it was Doak who broke in, since nothing was missing," he said, glancing over at Jake. The other detective nodded. "So what was he after? He wasn't trying to terrorize A.J. If he was, he'd have made sure she knew he was here."

"Yeah. He's getting desperate to find Mindy and Jamie. He must have been looking for their location."

"There's nothing here that could help him," A.J. said, savoring the comfort of leaning against Mac. "I don't keep any files at home."

"How about phone numbers or addresses? Do you keep shelter information here?" Mac asked.

"No." She shook her head. "I don't keep anything work-related at home. If I bring anything home with me, I always take it back the next day."

"That brings up another question," Mac said, his voice grim. "How did Doak know where you live?"

"You've had a regular parade of squad cars to and from this apartment," she said tartly. "He could have followed any one of them."

"And thank God they were here," he countered. "Otherwise Doak might have gotten in when you were home."

"Kids, kids, kids. Knock it off," Jake said. "Don't make me come over to that couch."

Mac scowled at him and settled his arm more firmly around her shoulders. "All right, *Dad*. Do you have any ideas?"

"Do you think there's any way Doak could have found out where Mindy or Jamie are?" A.J. asked.

"You're sure you don't keep that kind of info here?" Mac asked.

"Positive."

"You don't keep anything here that could identify the shelters or the hotel?"

"No. Nothing."

"Then it's hard to see what Doak could have learned."

"I make phone calls occasionally, but I don't keep phone numbers here, either."

"Does anyone call you at home?"

"Once in a while."

His arm tightened around her. "Did Mindy or Cissy call?"

"Cissy called a couple of times."

Mac and Jake leaped up at the same time. "Do you have caller ID?"

"Yes," she said, then she realized the implication. "Oh, no," she whispered. "Doak could have gotten the number of the hotel from my caller ID."

Mac nodded, his face grim. "He wouldn't have known it was Cissy, but he's a smart guy. He might have put two and two together."

Jake tossed her the phone. Her hand shook as she punched in the numbers. When Cissy answered, she exhaled.

"Cissy. Are you and Jamie all right?"

When Cissy told her they were fine, A.J. said, "I'm going to let you talk to Mac."

Mac took the phone. "Cissy, I don't want to scare you," he said. "But don't open your door for anyone until my partner and I get there. There's a slight possibility that Doak might know where you are."

He listened for a while, then shook his head. "No, I think you and Jamie will be fine. But we're going to move you to another hotel. Get your things packed and I'll explain when I get there."

He hung up the phone and said to Jake, "Let's go." He turned to A.J. "You're going to have to come with us. I'm not going to leave you here alone. And I don't want to wait until a patrol car gets here."

"All right."

Mac herded her out the door ahead of him, then

moved so she was between him and Jake. Walking between two large men would normally have made her nervous, she realized. But with Mac and Jake she felt safe. Their size was reassuring, not threatening.

As they waited for the elevator, Jake said, "So who was this witness that kept you at the country club?"

"One of the waiters. He'd been on vacation, visiting his family in Mexico. He didn't know about Helena until he got back to work today." Mac's lips thinned. "He saw Helena getting into a car with a man the night she disappeared. He's confident he can identify the man. And it sounds like Doak."

"Sounds like we have Doak wrapped up in a package with a nice bow on top."

"If we can find him."

The elevator arrived, the door opened and they stepped inside. The strong aroma of cleaning solution in the passenger compartment couldn't quite cover up the faint, acrid smell of tobacco smoke. The combination, along with her fears for Cissy and Jamie, made A.J. queasy.

The elevator door started to open on the first floor, but Mac pushed a button and kept it closed. "Cissy and Jamie are at the Tarrington Hotel. Room 423. I'll take A.J. and meet you there."

Jake glanced at A.J. "Want me to have a patrol car meet us there to keep an eye on A.J.?"

"Yeah."

Jake nodded and Mac opened the elevator door. A couple from the floor above her, evidently realizing they'd delayed the elevator, scowled at them as they walked out. When the man opened his mouth, Mac flashed his badge in the guy's face without breaking stride. A.J. saw the shocked look on her neighbor's face as they walked out the door.

"You shouldn't have flashed your badge like that," she said as they hurried to his car. "Now everyone in the building is going to think I've been arrested."

"Who the hell cares what they think?"

The barbed wire protecting her heart pinched a little tighter, the sharp points digging into her. "I care," she said quietly.

He froze, his hand on the car door, a stricken look on his face. "Hell, A.J. I didn't think. I'm sorry."

"It doesn't matter," she said as he got into the car. "Don't worry about it."

"Yeah, it does matter." He shoved his hand through his hair, then turned around and maneuvered the car out of its parking spot. "If it hurt you, it matters."

She studied her hands, clasped in her lap. "I have to get over it." She looked over at him. "Even Kate told me I have to get over it."

"You're a different person than you were fifteen years ago," Mac said softly. "You're one of the success stories. You've made something of yourself, done something with your life. You deserve to be able to let the past go."

She stared straight ahead out the windshield. "The past still matters to you," she said softly.

"I'm an idiot," he retorted. "A thick-headed, stubborn, blind idiot." He didn't look at her, but she saw his hands tighten on the steering wheel. "I should never have let you walk out of my house last night."

"But you did." She closed her eyes against the pain and regrets. "And I should have told you sooner about my past. But I didn't. So where does that leave us?"

"Hell if I know." He glanced over at her. "But I won't let you walk away from me next time."

"If there is a next time." She spoke so softly that she wasn't sure if he heard her above the droning of the engine. He shot her a sharp look, but before he could answer, he was parking the car at the curb. They'd arrived at the hotel.

"Where is that damn patrol car?" Mac muttered as he looked around.

Jake's car screeched to a halt at the curb behind them. He jumped out and hurried over to them. "It's going to be a while until a squad car gets here," he said with a worried look at A.J. "There's a bad accident on the other side of town and most of the cars are tied up."

Mac swore violently under his breath. When he looked at A.J., she saw both fear and wariness in his eyes.

"We have no choice," he finally said. "We can't leave her in the car. What if Doak shows up and sees her?"

"How about the manager's office?" Jake asked.

"That won't work." Mac glanced over at her. "Too accessible."

"Then we'll have to take her with us," Jake said.

"Are you out of your mind?" Mac shouted.

"What are the alternatives? Leave her in the car and make her a sitting duck? Let her lounge around in the lobby? You want to keep her safe, she stays with us."

Mac scowled, but it was clear he couldn't come up with another idea. "You will do exactly what Jake and I tell you to do," he said to A.J. "Do you understand?"

"I'm not an idiot," she said. "Of course I understand."

Mac got out of the car, his face grim. "All right. Let's get this over with."

CHAPTER TWENTY-ONE

"WHERE ARE WE GOING to take them?" Jake asked as they walked in the front door of the hotel.

"We'll figure that out in the car." Mac unsnapped the flap holding the gun in its holster under his left arm. "First priority is getting them away from here."

"Right." Jake unzipped the light jacket he wore and exposed his own gun. "Stairs or elevator?"

Mac didn't hesitate. "Stairs. Make sure no one's waiting there."

"Got it." Jake nodded at the exit sign above the steel door in front of them. "You take this one. I'll get the other stairwell. Fourth floor, right?"

"Right."

He watched until Jake disappeared around a corner, then turned to A.J. "You stay behind me. Don't say a thing. I need to listen. And you do what I tell you, instantly, without thinking about it." He studied her eyes, glad to see the uneasy fear in them. It would make her cautious.

"I understand." She nodded once, then licked her lips. "Mac," she began, but he held up his hand.

"The no-talking part starts right now."

She closed her mouth and nodded again. He thought he saw regret in her eyes and almost asked her what she wanted to say. But he forced himself to focus on his job.

"Follow me."

He eased open the fire door and stepped into the stairwell. Concrete steps rose above them, stark and utilitarian. The lightbulbs on each landing cast shadows on the stairs, and the gray paint on the railings was pitted and chipped.

He let the door close and stood for a moment, listening. He heard A.J. breathing softly behind him, standing perfectly still. He strained to hear, but no sounds drifted down the stairwell.

"All right," he whispered, reaching back blindly and grasping A.J.'s hand. "Let's go."

She clung to him as they climbed the stairs. He forced himself to ignore the sensation, ignore the rightness of her hand in his. Right now she was just an unwelcome civilian complication to his job. He couldn't afford to think of her any other way.

When they reached the fourth floor, he stopped and let go of A.J.'s hand. Before he could open the door, he heard a sharp crack. It sounded like wood splintering. When he heard a woman scream, he pushed through the door and ra d to Cissy and Jamie's room.

Sick fear swelled in his gut as he saw that the door was open, the frame broken. He pulled his gun from his holster and stepped through it.

"Well, well, well. Look who's here for the party."

Doak stood in the living room of the suite, holding a gun on Cissy, who had planted herself in front of Jamie. Tears ran down her face, but she faced Doak defiantly. Jamie's face was paper white, his eyes huge and terrified. He glanced over at Mac, his eyes accusing.

You promised, his eyes said. *You promised he wouldn't hurt me again.*

"Drop the gun, Doak," Mac said, his finger on the trigger of his gun.

"Now why would I want to do that?" He pressed the barrel of his gun against Cissy's head. "It looks like I'm holding all the cards here."

"You're not leaving this room," Mac said, his voice steady. "Don't make it worse for yourself."

"How could I possibly make it worse for myself? You've found that slut Helena's body, and thanks to Jamie you found my clothes." He glared at the boy. "He needs a lesson in how to keep his mouth shut."

"You kill Cissy or Jamie and you're looking at the death penalty," Mac said quietly, hating that he had to bargain with Doak. "Put the gun down and the D.A. might agree to life instead."

"You think I want to spend the rest of my life in prison?" Doak sneered. "I've got two 'get out of jail' cards, and I intend to use them. Either I walk away with Cissy and Jamie, or I'll kill them right now."

Out in the hall, A.J. gasped. Doak's head snapped around. "Who's out there?"

"There's no one out there," Mac answered. Sweat ran down his back and his sides.

"The hell there isn't." He jerked Cissy's head back and she yelped. "Come on in and join the party."

Stay there, he silently begged A.J. *Don't move.*

"Either you come in here or Cissy gets her brains splattered on the wall," Doak called.

A.J. stepped slowly into the room. Doak's eyes lit up.

"This is a pleasant surprise. How considerate of you to bring her to me, Detective. I was afraid I'd have to go find her myself." He gestured with the gun. "Come on over here, bitch."

"No." Mac angled his body so he was between Doak and A.J. "If you want a hostage, you take me. Cissy, Jamie and A.J. stay here."

"I don't think so, cop. I'm the one making the rules." He grabbed Cissy and yanked her against him. "Ms. Ferguson and I are going to have a lot of fun together."

He wrapped one arm around Cissy's neck and held the gun to her head. "Drop your gun, Detective."

Mac's hand tightened on his gun, anger burning in his gut. Cissy's terrified eyes pleaded with him to obey Doak. Slowly he set his gun on the floor. He could shoot Doak, but not before Doak could shoot Cissy.

"Now move away from the door," Doak ordered.

Mac reached behind him and grabbed A.J., pulling her behind him, then edged away from the door.

Doak grinned. "I don't think so, Detective." He pointed his gun at A.J. "You come over here."

Mac felt A.J. take a deep breath then step away from him. She took a tiny step toward Doak, then another.

"That's close enough," he ordered. Hatred flashed in his eyes. "Let's see you do your fancy martial-arts moves from there."

A.J. stood perfectly still. Suddenly Doak shoved Cissy back toward the couch. She stumbled and fell to the floor, and Doak lunged for A.J.

She managed to kick him once, but before she could kick him again, he had his arm around her throat and the gun to her head. "We're going to leave now," he said. "Don't follow us if you want to see her alive again."

As Doak edged A.J. toward the door, Mac prayed Jake was in the hall. Their only hope was to surprise Doak.

A scraping noise came from the hall and Doak jerked his head toward the door. At the same moment, A.J. dropped like a stone, slipping out of his hold. Without thinking, Mac leaped for her, covering her with his body.

"Hands up," Jake ordered from the doorway.

Mac felt her tremble beneath him and he edged her

toward the bedroom door, using his body as a barrier between her and Doak. Nothing else mattered, he realized. Nothing but keeping her safe.

"Drop the gun," Jake ordered. "Drop it and raise your arms."

Doak stood frozen, watching Jake, rage and hatred on his face.

"Do it! Now!"

Doak stared at him, the gun at his side. Slowly he lifted his hands, raising his arms above his head. But he still held the gun.

"I said drop the gun," Jake barked.

Doak kept raising his arms until they were above his head in the classic surrender position. But he still held the gun in his hand.

"One more chance, Talbott. Drop the gun."

Doak began lowering his right hand as if he were going to put the gun on the floor. Then his hand dropped and Jake's gun flashed. The gunshots echoed in the room, making Mac's ears ring.

Doak collapsed to the floor. Cissy let out a sharp cry and A.J. tensed beneath Mac.

"Are you all right?" she asked, trying to turn him to face her. "Did he shoot you?"

"I'm fine," he said, squeezing her hand then standing up. "Stay there for a moment."

He glanced over at Cissy and Jamie. The boy's aunt had pressed his head into her waist, blocking his view of his father. Mac caught her eye and jerked his head in the direction of the bedroom. Cissy understood his meaning and scooped Jamie into her arms, hurrying into the bedroom and closing the door softly behind them.

Jake stood motionless in the doorway, his gun steady in his hand as he glanced at Mac. "Check him."

Mac strode over to Doak and used his foot to push the gun out of his reach. Then he bent over the fallen man and pressed his fingers to Doak's throat.

"He's gone," he said briefly, looking up at Jake.

Jake relaxed his stance and started to slip his gun into his holster. Then he hesitated. "You want to take this?" he asked Mac, holding his gun out to his partner, butt first.

"Hell, no," Mac said instantly. "That was a righteous shooting. There were three civilians at risk."

Jake hesitated, his eyes grim. Then he nodded once and put the gun back in its holster. "I'll call it in."

Mac knelt on the floor, next to where A.J. sat. "Are you all right?" he asked in a low voice.

"I'm fine," she said, standing up slowly. Her voice was shaky and her face was bleached white.

Mac grabbed her shoulders. "You don't look fine."

She drew a deep, trembling breath as she glanced at Doak. She immediately looked away. "Sorry. Some ugly memories."

Mac cursed himself for his insensitivity. "I should

have thought of that." He folded her into his arms, closed his eyes as he felt her heart beating against his. She clutched him tightly, holding him as if nothing else mattered. He brushed his lips over her hair, pulled her closer into his embrace.

"Knock it off, McDougal." Jake's voice was sharp. "We've got a little work to do here."

Mac eased away from her. "Let's get you in the bedroom with Cissy and Jamie."

She'd wrapped her arms around herself as if cold. "Yes. They probably could use some help."

"You're the one who needs help," he said roughly, giving her shoulders a shake. "Can't you think of yourself first for once?"

The glazed look began to disappear from A.J.'s eyes. "Thank you, Mac, but it will help to have something to do. It will help to focus on my job." She swallowed and tried again to look at Doak's body, but she couldn't. "Cissy and Jamie are going to need a lot of help in the next few weeks."

"Who's going to help you?" he asked.

"I can take care of myself," she answered.

"I know you can," he said, brushing her hair away from her face. "But you shouldn't have to."

She gave him a weary smile. "I've learned it's better not to depend on anyone but myself."

Mac started to lead her toward the closed bedroom door, but she pulled gently away and looked over at

Jake. "You did the right thing," she said to him. "Doak would have killed all of us."

Jake's face was gray but he gave her a tight nod. "Thanks. We'll see if the Police Board agrees."

Mac heard the ping as the elevator arrived, then footsteps pounded down the hall. Mac urged her toward the closed bedroom door. "You and Cissy are going to have to answer a few questions. Are you okay with that?"

"Of course. And I'm sure Cissy is fine with it, too. As long as one of us can stay with Jamie."

"That won't be a problem." He touched her arm. "We'll talk later, A.J."

She nodded, then closed the bedroom door quietly. He stared at it for a moment, feeling the invisible wall that had sprung up between them, regretting it, hating it. But as uniformed police officers ran into the room, he forced himself to put A.J. out of his head.

CHAPTER TWENTY-TWO

A.J. WALKED INTO THE STATION the next morning, anticipation humming through her. It fizzled when she saw Mac's unoccupied desk. The same files were scattered across its surface, his chair was in the same position as it had been the day before. He had obviously not been back in the office since yesterday.

Of course he hadn't, she reassured herself. There would be a lot of details to take care of. A lot of questions to answer. And a lot of loose ends that needed to be tied up.

"He hasn't been in yet," Jake said from the next desk.

She jerked her head up, embarrassed that her first instinct was to look for Mac, ashamed that she hadn't spoken to Jake first.

"It's okay, A.J.," Jake said. "I haven't heard from the knucklehead, either."

She rested her hip on the edge of Mac's desk and tried to push him out of her mind. "How are you doing, Jake?"

"Me? I'm happy as a pig in mud. We cleared the Talbott case and I get a few free days of vacation."

She felt a rush of affection for Jake. "You talk a good game, Donovan, but you don't fool me. You're a good man. Shooting Doak was tough for you."

"If I hadn't killed him, he would have shot everyone in that room." Jake's voice was flat. "I did what I was supposed to do."

"You're right. It was a justified shooting and you had no choice. That doesn't make it any easier."

"Yeah, well, I'm going to have plenty of time to think about it."

"Why?" She walked over to his desk and pulled up a chair. "All you have to do is talk to Dr. McGinnis. I know Kira. She's a very good psychologist. She'll get you back on the street as soon as possible."

Jake spun his chair around so she couldn't see his face. "Only after I spill my guts to her."

"What's so tough about that?" A.J. asked. "You tell her what happened, she makes sure you're dealing with it, she gives you back your badge and your gun."

Tension hovered in the air, startling A.J. Jake wasn't normally tightly wound.

"I don't like shrinks," he said in a low voice.

"Ouch, Jake," she said with a grin. "That really hits below the belt."

He looked at her. His eyes weren't laughing, as they usually were, and his mouth was a thin, grim line. "For

God's sake, A.J., I'm not talking about you," he said. "I mean I don't like *talking* to them."

"You've sure been putting up a good front, then, for the past couple of years."

His mouth softened. "You know what I mean, A.J. I don't like seeing them in a professional sense."

"Don't be a baby, Jake. Kira is easy to talk to. I'll tell her to be gentle with you."

She saw shutters come down in his eyes. "You're certainly chipper this morning," he said with a forced smile. "You sure you haven't seen Mac?"

"Not yet," she said, keeping the smile pasted to her face. "I'll catch up with him later. I have a lot to do this morning."

"Such as?"

"Mindy and Jamie are moving back into their house today. It's not going to be easy for either of them, and I want to be there in case they need help dealing with it."

Jake gave her a real smile, but there were still lines of strain around his eyes. "You take good care of people. That's why we're all crazy about you. Even though you have serious head-doctor tendencies."

He sat up in his chair. "Speaking of doing a great job, Jeanine Jamison was here earlier this morning. She left this for you." He handed her a small, brightly wrapped package. "She said to say thanks."

A.J. picked it up, felt the outline of a small book.

"How are they doing?" Jake asked.

A.J. opened the gift and let her fingers skim over the cover. It was a book of Walt Whitman poems. "I think they're going to be fine," she said with a smile. "Todd is making progress with his therapist and Jeanine is seeing someone, too. The last time I talked to Jeanine, she sounded almost giddy. Sometimes there *are* happy endings."

"I hope so," Jake said, his eyes bleak.

"HEY, BUDDY, HOW ARE YOU DOING?" Mac asked Jamie Talbott. The boy stood in the kitchen of his home, wearing a red Power Rangers backpack and clutching a small brown teddy bear to his chest. His mouth trembled as he looked toward the living room.

Mac crouched in front of him, blocking his view of the other room. "What's this guy's name?" he asked, nodding at the teddy bear.

Jamie looked down at the bear. One of its ears was torn, and he rubbed it between his fingers. "Thomas," he whispered.

"Does Thomas like to play Transformers?" Mac asked.

Jamie slowly shook his head. "He's afraid of them."

"Why is that?" Mac settled on the floor in front of Jamie.

"Transformers yell when they fight. Thomas gets scared."

Mac pretended to tickle the teddy bear's foot. "Would Thomas come and play with us if the Transformers promised not to yell?"

Jamie looked at him with faint hope. "Maybe."

"Do you want to go see?" Mac stood up and held out his hand. After a long moment, Jamie slid his tiny fingers against Mac's palm. "Okay."

Someone sniffled, and Mac looked up to find Mindy, Cissy and A.J. watching him. A.J. smiled, her eyes glistening. "Hello, Mac," she said quietly.

"Wh-when did you get here?" he said, stumbling over his tongue.

"While you were talking to Jamie." Her eyes filled with tenderness as she watched him. "I didn't know you'd be here this morning."

"Jamie has the best toys. Where else would I go if I wanted to play Transformers?"

A.J.'s smile trembled, but before she could say anything, Mindy touched her arm and said, "Isn't Mac wonderful with Jamie?"

A.J. held his gaze for a long moment. "Yes, he is."

He wanted to reach out for A.J., to reconnect with her, but he didn't know how to do it.

He wasn't here for A.J., he told himself. The faint echo of relief that slithered through him shamed him, but he pushed it away. He was here for Jamie.

"How about it, buddy? Should we go up to your room to play?"

Jamie's hand tightened in Mac's, and he nodded.

They started to climb the stairs together and Jamie kept his head carefully turned away from the living room where brightly colored pieces of plastic were crushed into the carpet.

"My dad broke those," Jamie said. His voice startled Mac, and he cursed himself for drawing the boy's attention to the destruction.

"Your dad did some bad things, Jamie." Mac glanced over his shoulder for A.J. This was her department.

"My mom said he was sick."

"She's right," he answered. "Your dad was very sick."

Jamie held his hand more tightly as they got to the top of the stairs and walked down the hall. He opened a door. "This is my room." The stale smell of a room left unused for a while drifted out.

"It's a cool room, Jamie," Mac said, looking around at the stuffed animals on the bed, the *Star Wars* figures on the dresser and the rows of books in the bookcase.

"Do you want to play with Autobot and Decepticon again?" Jamie asked, pulling two Transformers out of his backpack. "Last time they fought the bad guys together. They usually fight each other."

"Yeah. I bet they'll gang up on the bad guys again."

He listened for A.J.'s steps on the stairs, but all he heard was the faint murmur of voices from the first floor. He forced himself to concentrate on Jamie.

"THANK YOU FOR PLAYING with Jamie," Mindy Talbott said when he came downstairs an hour later. "You're all he's talked about since yesterday."

"He's a great kid," Mac said, his voice gruff. He looked for A.J., but she was gone.

Mindy gave him a wistful smile. "You'll be a wonderful father, Mac."

Mac shoved his hands into his pockets and shrugged. "I don't know about that."

Mindy's smile deepened. "A.J. is a very lucky woman."

Desperation clutched at Mac. *He* would be the lucky one. If he could figure out a way to tell A.J. how he felt. If he could find a way to get past his fear and hesitation. If he could convince her to take a chance on him.

He managed to smile. "A.J. is very special."

Mindy touched his arm. "You're both very special. Take care of each other."

He wanted to take care of A.J., he thought as he walked to his truck. He just didn't know how to do it.

When he got back to the station, he found himself walking toward Kira McGinnis's office. He had to visit the psychologist anyway, he told himself. It was department regulation after being involved in a fatal shooting. He might as well get it over with.

Fifteen minutes later, Mac sat stiffly in the chair in

Kira McGinnis's office, nerves making his foot jump. "You need to sign me off on the Talbott shooting," he said.

Kira tilted her head as she watched him. "I'm surprised you came to me voluntarily," she said, speculation in her eyes. "I usually have to drag you guys in here, kicking and screaming."

Mac shrugged. "I wanted to get it over with."

"Cops have said a lot of things to me, but that's a first," she said with a grin. "Why don't you tell me your version of what happened yesterday."

Mac recounted the events in an even voice while Kira took notes. After fifteen minutes, she nodded.

"In your judgment, was Doak Talbott an immediate threat to you, your partner or the civilians present?"

"Yes. I'm convinced he would have shot all of us."

She asked several more questions, then put her pen down. "My recommendation to the oversight board will be that this was a justified shooting. You won't have any problems with this one."

"Thanks, doc," Mac said. He cleared his throat, desperately searching for a way to bring up what he really wanted to talk about.

Kira set her pen down and leaned back in her chair. "Is something else bothering you, Mac?"

He looked away from her. "Is it that obvious?"

"I know you didn't come in here to talk about Doak."

"She's driving me crazy," he muttered. "And I can't figure out what to do about it."

"Who is *she*, Mac?" she asked softly.

He scowled at her. "Don't tell me you haven't heard the gossip."

"I try not to listen to that. But I'm yours for the next forty minutes. I'd like to help you."

He jumped to his feet and stared out the window into the parking lot. His eyes went to the spot where A.J. parked her car. It was empty.

Take it easy, he told himself. *Doak is gone. She's okay.*

"This is hard for me," he muttered.

"I know." The doctor's voice was gentle. "It's hard to talk about your fears. It's very courageous to admit you need help."

"I screwed up, doc. Big time." He shoved his hands into his pockets, stared blindly out the window. "I need A.J. in my life. But I don't know how to get her there. I can't take that step."

He faced the psychologist. "I have no idea what to do next. I've never gotten this far with a woman."

Kira grinned, her eyes crinkling at the corners. "That's not the way I've heard it, Mac. I thought you got just about anything you wanted from your women."

He couldn't stop the answering grin. "Very funny, doc. You must be taking lessons from Donovan." He roamed the office, picking up a statue of a child fishing. He set it down, stared at a picture of a young girl playing softball. Finally he turned to look at her.

"I feel like an ass, spilling my guts to a shrink."

"Would you rather go to McGonigle's and talk to a friend over a beer? Would that make it easier for you?"

"Yeah," he said, taking a deep breath. "Let's go to McGonigle's. I could use a drink."

A.J. CLOSED THE DOOR to her apartment and leaned against it, the silence stabbing into her like tiny knives. Her apartment had never felt lonely before. She'd always thought of it as her refuge. But tonight the quiet swelled until she couldn't bear it.

She turned on the television to end the silence, to keep herself from thinking of what might have been. Pictures of Mac with Jamie Talbott had played in her head all day long. He'd been so tender with Jamie, so careful.

He'd known exactly the right things to say.

It had made her ache for what could have been. For the sight of Mac playing with *their* children. For the tenderness he would have shown with *their* son or daughter.

No matter how much she wanted it, it wasn't going to happen. She was an adult. No one had to spell it out for her. Mac's avoidance of her since Doak had been killed said everything.

Mac meant what he'd said about relationships. He wasn't interested in making a commitment.

And even if he wanted to make a commitment, her past stood in the way.

Mac was born to be a detective. Not only did he love what he did, but he was one of the best at his job. There was no way she'd take that away from him.

And the rules were very clear for police officers in Riverton—they weren't allowed to associate with people who had been convicted of a felony.

She poured herself a glass of wine and went to get changed. Her heart bled a little as she slipped into the pajamas that had fired Mac's blood, but she forced herself to do it anyway. She would get over him, she vowed.

It would just take a long time.

The rest of your life, a tiny voice whispered, but she pushed the thought away.

She was watching the Lifetime channel when someone knocked on her door. Setting down her glass of wine, she grabbed a robe from the bedroom. "Who is it?" she called.

"It's Mac."

Her heart swooped in her chest then began battering her ribs. She took a deep breath, plastered an impersonal smile firmly on her face and opened the door.

"Come in," she said.

He stepped past her, swept his gaze over her from the top of her head, over her bathrobe and down to her bare feet. She curled her toes and waited for him to look up.

"Hello, A.J."

His low voice strummed against her nerves, and she cinched the belt of her robe tighter. "Hi, Mac. How's the wrap-up of the case going?" she said, her voice bright.

He pushed the door closed. "I don't want to talk about this case."

"No? Then what do you want?"

He studied her, a tiny smile flickering around his mouth. "You asked me that once before," he said. "Are you looking for the same answer?"

Memories of that night washed over her. Mac's mouth on her, his hands stroking her body, her mindless response to him, his overwhelming need for her. She stepped back—right into the wall. Heat flooded her cheeks as she jerked away from it. "I'm not looking for anything."

"Is that right?" He moved closer, trapping her. The heat from his body surrounded her, and her mouth trembled.

"You don't owe me anything, Mac."

"You're wrong," he said. "I owe you a lot of things." He braced his hands on the wall next to her head. "I owe you an explanation of what's happened in the case since you walked out of that hotel room."

"I've been wondering about that," she managed to say.

He watched her with hooded eyes. "I owe you a thank you for taking care of Mindy and Jamie."

She swallowed hard, wished he would back away. "That's my job."

"I owe you an apology for not telling you sooner."

He bent closer to her and she ducked her head, sliding under his arm and away from him.

"Don't worry about it," she said, trying to keep her voice brisk and nonchalant. "I know you've been busy."

She needed to get him out of here. She was afraid if he stayed, she'd beg. And she wouldn't embarrass him like that. Rolling her shoulders, she said, "Thanks for coming by to fill me in.

"Are you nervous about something, A.J.? You're acting jittery."

"What would I be nervous about?" She licked her lips. "You just surprised me, that's all. I wasn't expecting you. It's late and I was getting ready for bed." Her hands clutched the lapels of her robe.

"Don't let me stop you," he murmured, stepping close again. She curled her fingers into the fleece lining the pockets.

Why wouldn't he just go? "I assume all the ends in the case have been tied up," she said. "Were you able to prove that Doak killed Helena Tripp?"

"Yeah. It was her blood on the shirt he buried. And she had his skin beneath her fingernails."

"Good," she said struggling to give him an impersonal smile. "I'm glad you were able to clear the case."

"Me, too. There are other things I need to concentrate on."

She refused to hope. "Have you gotten new cases already?" she asked, desperate for an innocuous topic of conversation.

"Nope. Not until Jake sees Kira McGinnis and gets cleared. Aren't you going to ask me what I needed to concentrate on?"

"All right, I'll humor you," she whispered. "What do you need to concentrate on?"

"You, A.J. I need to concentrate on you."

"No," she whispered. "It's all right. I've put our little 'thing' behind me. You don't need to rehash it."

His eyes darkened, heated. "Really, A.J.? You've put it behind you? You've forgotten how we are together? I haven't forgotten a thing. I can't."

No, she cried silently. *I haven't forgotten either.* "Why wouldn't I try to forget? You told me all along how you felt about relationships. About commitments." Her chest rose and fell as she drew in a hard, ragged breath. He stared at the front of her robe.

"I did, didn't I?" He dragged his gaze up to hers. "I was a damn fool."

He closed his hands over her shoulders, pulled her to him. "As well as a coward. I wanted to take what you were offering the other night, when you came to me. I needed you so much. But I was afraid, so I let you go. I won't do that again."

He cupped her face in his hand. "I love you, A.J. I fought like hell when I figured that out. I didn't want to love you. I didn't want you to matter so much."

His mouth twisted. "You terrified me, sweetheart. I didn't want to bare myself to you, to open up and let you see everything inside me, the ugly parts of myself I kept hidden. Because I knew that if I did, you wouldn't want anything to do with me."

"Mac," she said. "That's not—"

"Shhh." He put his hand on her mouth, let it linger there. "I had to make a choice, A.J. I could stay away from you and protect myself. Not let you hurt me. Not have to bare my soul to you."

He slowly traced her lips with a fingertip. She wanted to feel his body against hers, feel his heat and passion and desire.

Her body cried out in protest when he took his finger away from her lips. "Or I could come to you, tell you I loved you, hope that you loved me, too. Hope that you didn't laugh at me."

He slid his hands down her arms. "You know what I figured out?"

"What?" she whispered, unable to look away from him.

"There wasn't a choice after all. I could no more stay away from you than I could stop breathing. You're my life, A.J."

"Oh, Mac." She lifted her hands to his face, felt her throat swell with tears. "I love you, too. You're my life, my heart, my soul. You're everything. I'll never forget you."

"I hope you won't forget your husband. Marry me, A.J. Have children with me, grow old with me. Let me love you for the rest of your life."

"Don't, Mac." Her voice caught on a sob. "Don't make this any harder for me than it already is. You know I can't marry you."

"Why not?"

"I'm still a felon. And you're still a cop."

"You were a child who protected herself," he said fiercely. "You're no more a felon than I am."

"There are rules," she said. "Police departments are big on rules."

"I don't give a damn about the rules. And if anyone in Riverton does, there are plenty of other police departments in the Chicago area." He pressed a kiss against her mouth. "Your past won't affect our future. I won't let it. I don't want to hear you say 'felon' again."

Happiness filled every part of her. "Or what, McDougal? You'll spank me?"

His eyes darkened even more. "Oh, yeah, sweetheart. I knew you were a very naughty girl."

"Only with you, Mac."

She slid her fingers beneath his shirt, skimming her palms over his chest. But he removed her hands, held them between his.

"I can't think when you touch me, sweetheart. And we need to talk about something else." He brushed his mouth across hers. "You know I don't have a good relationship with my parents. But I want them to be part of my life. Part of our lives. Will you be able to deal with that?"

"Of course I can," she said. Her mouth curved into a smile. "I doubt that I'm your parents' idea of the perfect woman for you, but I'm glad you want to reach out to them."

He grinned at her, twisted one of her curls around his finger. "My father thinks you're perfect for me."

"Right." She rolled her eyes. "A girl from the wrong side of town? Who doesn't have a 'real' name? I wasn't born yesterday, McDougal."

"He told me so."

"Is that right?"

"Maybe not in so many words. But that's what he meant. When he gave me the information about Doak, he said he didn't want Doak to hurt you again. Because he knew I cared about you. He asked me to bring you over for dinner."

He brought her hands to his mouth, pressed a kiss into each palm. "Will you come with me to visit them?"

"Without hesitation."

"My father made the first move. He came to me. I want to put the bitterness behind us." His grip tightened on her hands. "When I was growing up, we used to play golf together. Maybe we can play some golf again."

"That sounds perfect." She smiled through the tears

that filled her eyes. "He's trying to patch your relationship. I'm glad you're trying, too."

She leaned in to kiss him, but he held her back. "You still haven't answered my question, you know."

"Ask me again, Mac," she murmured against his mouth.

"Will you marry me, A.J.? Do you love me enough to have children with me, to grow old with me?" His mouth curved into a smile against hers. "Do you love me enough to put up with my temper and my family?"

"Yes, Mac." She lifted her face, let the tears fall. "Yes, I'll marry you. I want to make a life with you. I can't live without you. We're putting all the bad memories from our childhoods behind us, Mac. From now on, the only memories we make will be good ones." She curled her arms around his neck. "I'm even looking forward to our fights."

"Why is that?"

"I'm really going to enjoy kissing and making up."

She felt him smile against her neck. "Maybe we should have a fight right now."

"I'd rather skip right to the making up part."

"I have a better idea."

"What's that?" she asked, loving the solid feel of his chest against hers.

"We'll get married backward."

She leaned away from him. "What?"

"I can't wait until after we're married for the rest of

our life to begin." He bent his head, kissed her until she throbbed in his arms. "I'm definitely not waiting to start the honeymoon."

"Yes," she whispered. "I can't wait another second. The rest of our life starts right now."

He searched for her mouth, kissed her. Tenderness caught fire, ignited into hot, aching need. He tugged at the belt of her robe, pulled it open. His eyes darkened when he saw her pajamas.

"Did you wear those for me?" His voice was dark and husky.

"I was thinking of you when I put them on," she answered. "Wishing you were here… To take them off me."

He slid his finger into the waistband, tugged gently. "Sweetheart, I live to serve."

SUDDENLY A PARENT

FAMILY AT LAST
by K.N. Casper

Harlequin Superromance #1292

Adoption is a life-altering commitment.
Especially when you're single. And your new
son doesn't speak your language. But when
Jarrod hires Soviet-born linguist Nina Lockhart
to teach Sasha English, he has no idea
how complicated his life is about to become.

*Available in August 2005
wherever Harlequin books are sold.*

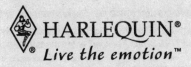

AMERICAN *Romance*

is happy to bring you
a new 3-book series by

Dianne Castell

Forty & Fabulous

Here are three very funny books
about three women who have grown up
together in Whistler's Bend, Montana.
These friends are turning forty and are
struggling to deal with it. But who said
you can't be forty and fabulous?

A FABULOUS WIFE
(#1077, August 2005)

A FABULOUS HUSBAND
(#1088, October 2005)

A FABULOUS WEDDING
(#1095, December 2005)

Available wherever Harlequin books are sold.

HARFF0705

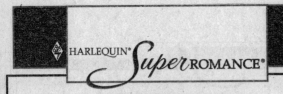

HARLEQUIN *Super* ROMANCE®

HOMETOWN
U.S.A.

DEAR CORDELIA
by Pamela Ford

Harlequin Superromance #1291

"Dear Cordelia" is Liza Dunnigan's ticket out
of the food section. If she can score an interview
with the reclusive columnist, she'll land an
investigative reporter job and change her boring,
predictable life. She just has to get past
Cordelia's publicist, Jack Graham, hiding
her true intentions to get what she needs.
But Jack is hiding something, too....

*Available in August 2005
wherever Harlequin books are sold.*

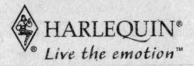

HARLEQUIN®
Live the emotion™

ANOTHER WOMAN'S SON

by Anna Adams

Harlequin Superromance #1294

**The truth should set you free.
Sometimes it just tightens the trap.**

Three months ago Isabel Barker's life came crashing down after her husband confessed he loved another woman—Isabel's sister—and that they'd had a son together. No one else, including her sister's husband, Ben, knows the truth about the baby. When her sister and her husband are killed, Tony is left with Ben, and Isabel wonders whether she should tell the truth. She knows Ben will never forgive her if her honesty costs him his son.

*Available in August 2005
wherever Harlequin books are sold.*

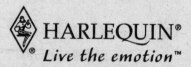

HARLEQUIN®
Live the emotion™